TIME SCIENCE!

EDITED BY: DR. ADAM TOMLINSON

ISBN: 978-1-7778910-0-8

This is a work of fiction. Names, characters, places, and incidents are the product of the author's imagination or used fictitiously. Any resemblance to any persons, living or dead, events, or locals is entirely coincidental.

info@timesciencebooks.com

ALSO BY DR. ADAM TOMLINSON

Advanced Quantum Chromodynamics
The Philosophy and Physics of Chemoreception
Building a Better Particle Accelerator: Tips and Tricks
The Biology of Pseudocalanus
Quantum Entanglement: Spooky Action Up Close?
Hilarious Dendrochronology Jokes
More Hilarious Dendrochronology Jokes

CONTENTS

"Anyone who has never made a mistake
has never tried anything new."

— Albert Einstein

For my fellow scientists.

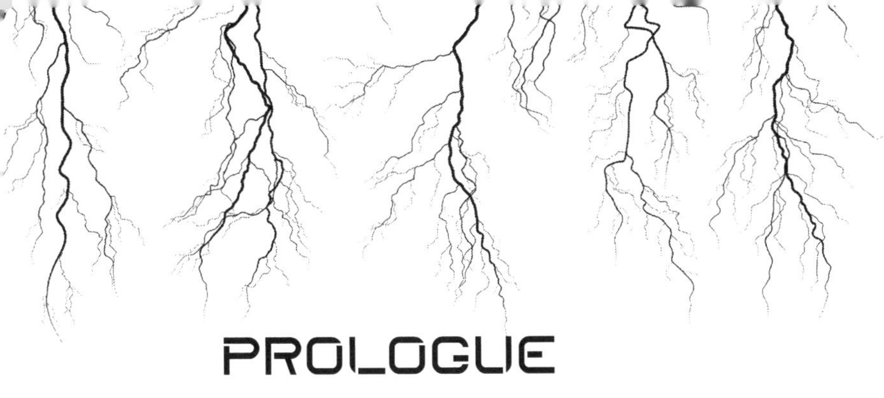

PROLOGUE

It was an ordinary day. I was lifting weights and making charitable donations when I was blinded by a flash of light above the infinity pool. Before my eyes could adjust, I heard the unmistakable clatter of AirPods bouncing off Peruvian marble, followed by the fluttering of falling pages, and once again capable of sight, I saw them. The media that form the basis of this book. Wisdom from the future, which has, by means far too complex to explain in a brief prologue written for a general audience, fallen back in time, landing directly at my feet. Being naturally curious, it was not long before I devoured the lot, finding the science to be sound and the arguments convincing beyond any standard of doubt. And though the following prophesizes a future of anguish and bloodshed, it's not up to me to play the nanny's role. Even the most innocuous monkey's paw will eventually clench into a fist.

- Dr. Adam Tomlinson

THE MACHINE

By

Dr. Penny Black

Editor's Note: Though it may surprise some, it should be noted that AirPods constantly read and record the user's mind. Every thought, feeling and impulse every "customer" ever had. Why? So this very private information can, at best, be sold to advertisers, and, at worst... well, it's best not to think about it. Especially if you're wearing AirPods. As for my means of extrapolating the data, my lawyers have advised me to keep mum on my methodology given its tendency to wade into proprietary waters and the Turtleneck Company's reputation for aggressive litigation.

April 2, 2024

6:39

I arrive early, being unable to sleep, thinking I'll pass some time in the cafeteria sipping coffee, only to find the machine has broken down overnight.

I try not to take it as a sign.

I call over my droopy-faced assistant, Thomas, a 17-year-old nephew-to-somebody who shrouds a complete lack of intellect, competence or talent under a three-layer veil of boyish charm, a penchant for platitudes and proclivity for wearing hats with interesting backstories. Today, he wears a mustard yellow beret bartered from the CFO of a lesbian biker gang at last year's Mardi Gras in exchange for a bag of hallucinogenic mushrooms purchased on sale at Woolworths.

"Thomas," I say, "I need some Gloria Jeans, pronto. Double latte."

"You got it, boss!" he replies, already heading for the door.

"And a shot of espresso."

He pauses. "So why don't you just get-"

"Just..." I hold up a hand and scrunch my shoulders in uninviting agitation. Of course, it would make more sense to get a triple, but I'm no glutton, and more importantly, I don't want to be perceived as one. He catches my drift and exits, clumsily brushing against an illustrated portrait of King George V depicted in a sharp naval uniform, causing it to sway slightly as if shaking his head in royal disapproval.

I try not to take it as a sign.

6:45

My attempt to distract myself by scrolling through news – politics, sports, something about a rampaging forest fire – has failed, so I unroll my blueprints, which I've double-checked a thousand times, and it's far too late for changes, but I pour over them anyway.

6:49

Thomas has not returned. I type half an admonishing text which I delete. I must not let him know how much real estate his buffoonery occupies rent-free in my mind.

6:51

The first of the laborers arrive. We make small talk about the future. He's looking forward to a hefty pay raise, wants to marry his significant other, maybe start a family. Throughout, he tries repeatedly and with growing frustration to operate the coffee machine. I'd tell him it's broken, but some lessons are best learned from experience. Where the hell is Thomas? I check my pulse. It's accelerating. Breathe, Penny, breathe.

6:55

Thomas has finally returned munching a half-eaten chicken breast and pesto panini sandwich I don't recall authorizing; however, also carrying a triple espresso. Bless his simple heart. I regret all the cruel things I've thought about him. Only 66 minutes to go. Thomas is saying Gloria Jeans isn't what it once was, but I disagree, finishing my beverage in three giant gulps. Delicious. I check my phone, note the time, and resolve to pretend to drink it for another 10 minutes so as not to appear gluttonous.

6:57

I toss the empty cup in the trash. Thomas raises his eyebrows in a way that all but screams "glutton!", and the cruel thoughts about him return.

7:01

I can't sit here another hour. I don't know why I thought a triple latte would help my anxiety. I feel like a mafia don on the day of their daughter's wedding as one laborer after another approaches thanking me for my work. I excuse myself and exit.

7:03

My office offers sanctuary from the well-wishers but not my own insecurities. How did I get here? Damn near 40. House mortgaged to the hilt. Growing up, I didn't want to be an engineer, let alone head a team of them. The ocean was my one true love, and as a grom, I planned, as soon as I was legally able, to move to some place like Darwin, take on menial employment. Anything I could stop thinking about at day's end. Maybe even something I enjoyed. Like Great Barrier Reef snorkel tours or feral cat hunts. Things that could make an ecological contribution to our great nation as well.

My knee bounces involuntarily as I await my creation's arrival. The Machine. The trades are calling it not just the next generation, but the last. High praise, but not undeserved. The key, as with all my work, is efficiency, a value most engineers ignore in pursuit of pointless idiosyncrasy. Case in point, John Bradfield's initial design of the Sydney Harbor Bridge, which included a bus stop in the middle, a seemingly innocent quirk that grows more sinister the more you think about it. My design, however, is the epitome of efficiency. Not just its internal machinery, but its command over the entire production chain as determined by my patented artificial intelligence driven decision making tree.

7:45

The Machine is on its way and should arrive approximately as scheduled, nearing the end of its 160-kilometer trek from a factory just outside Newcastle, a converted WWII-era shipyard. There, the illustrious HMAS Canberra underwent crucial repairs before triumphantly setting sail for the Battle of Savo Island and becoming among the first casualties of Japanese gunships. I went down more than a few nautical rabbit holes during the research process. While a few components are making the trek by truck, the Machine is far too massive for such conventional means. So, it is traveling via custom-built railway, similar to that the Yankees used to transport their space shuttle to its launch pad at Kennedy Space Center, so named after the one-term president famous for having lunched with Prime Minister Robert Menzies in 1963. The news provides some relief, but not much. Getting it here is the easy part. Whether or not it works is the question. If it doesn't, everyone here loses their job. Except, most of the others will find fast work elsewhere. I, however, will be ruined.

I stare at the wall clock carved into the shape of our great nation with an image of anthropologist Baldwin Spencer painted on it, a reference that's either cringingly on the nose or bafflingly obscure depending on if you work here. I should have left 10 minutes ago. I check my phone. There are 12 messages from Thomas. None contain words. Just faces. But I can tell by how the expressions go from tear-sheddingly happy to face-burningly nonplussed it's time to go.

7:59

It's all starting to feel real. Like that time, online, I found photos of my ex-lover, Laird, vacationing in Bali with that whore Nadine. I rush down a hallway lined with images of royal figures, domestic flora and fauna, and important national monuments, but they're an unregistered peripheral blur in my haste. A thousand thoughts race through my mind, none welcome or helpful, and for the umpteenth time today, I tell myself *relax*. I should not have had that triple latte. Especially after the whole pot of coffee and handful of caffeine pills I had earlier at home. Arriving at the huge double doors, recently painted matte black (a nice touch), I take a deep breath. Collect myself. Toss them open wide.

8:01

I'm struck by the barrenness of the factory floor. Usually, it's littered with slitter rewinders, core cutters, balers, shredders, compressors and sheeters, but now, it's empty except for several truckloads of unmarked crates stacked around the loading dock. Before I can inspect them, however, I am accosted by my boss, Mr. Fanning, who insists on being called "Mick", and presently wears a bright orange hard hat and yellow-tinged safety goggles he manages to pull off in a hipsterish way that infuriates me. "Morning, slow-poke!" he says with a mix of passive aggression and Gold Coast charm. I ignore both to the extent possible. "Should be here soon, your Machine. Which is good news, yeah?"

I nod.

"Spot of trouble *en route,* though. Nothing major. Just a few protesties."

"Environmentalists?" I say too loudly but needing an outlet lest my eye starts doing that thing.

"No, actually. Collectors!" He sounds surprised, but I'm not. It was inevitable that cliquey gaggle of dorks would eventually put two and two together and get something approximating four. To hell with them. If they don't like our contribution to the supply, they can get on their metaphorical dork horses and ramp up demand. Just recruit more dorks.

Thomas approaches wearing the same safety accoutrements as Mr. Fanning – sorry, Mick! – and carrying a set for me. He also has a turtle head of snot poking from his nose, and I make a mental note to snarkily refer to his birth cohort as Generation Z-*Minus* in some future social setting. I don the hardhat and goggles and see the world as if looking through a jar of pig urine. I want this to be over. The whole ordeal. With any luck, a year from now, I'll be living on a beach relaxing with my thoughts and a tanned, muscular stud.

8:15

Laborers carrying tablets scroll down lists, shouting instructions to laborers wielding tools ranging from wrenches to the most complex measuring devices available outside the military. The expense is practically tangible. The land. Transportation. Materials. Laborers. Tearing down a 35-meter tall load-bearing wall. It's one thing to peruse a spreadsheet with an enormous number at the bottom, it's quite another to see it all in action.

10:37

Finally, after all these years and the sacrifices I've made, I see the Machine. Looming magnificently in the distance. Moving silently as if under its own power, an electric locomotive pushing at 5 kph from behind. For some reason, I always pictured the engine up front. Not that that would make sense. It doesn't. It would be absurd. That's just what popped in my head. God, it's stunning. A hulking mass of strategically selected metals, plastics, carbon fiber and circuitry all painted matte black, making it seem even heavier than its almost 18 million kilograms. I fiddle excitedly with my AirPods.

10:38

My throat constricts as it dawns on me: we forgot to reinforce the floor! The Machine will grind the concrete into dust! But of course, this has already been done and to my satisfaction.

11:22

The Machine enters the building, and in less than half an hour, it is in place, and the laborers get to work. Slowly drawing back the protective layers of cellophane, some sheets broad enough to power a four-masted Barque Sedov in a 15-knot breeze. Next comes the attachment of wires, hoses, pipes, etc. I hear rumbling and know the floor beneath the Machine is opening to facilitate still more attachments, including the main power source, a cable thicker than an oil barrel.

13:21

Thomas asks if I'd like him to make a Gloria Jeans run. Can't he tell my nerves are shot and my blood pressure borderline volcanic? Is he trying to kill me? "Sure," I say, already feeling regret as I watch him jog away, lower legs flopping like he doesn't have knees.

April 28

13:23

So much vomiting lately. Flushing the staff room toilet two, three even four times, trusting my coworkers' limited imaginations to arrive upon less sordid conclusions than the truth. We lost an entire week because of washers. Washers! Despite being very clear with my instructions, an American company, Talleyrand Washers, sent $200,000 worth of the little round bastards that didn't fit because they were in inches. Inches! And they have "Talleyrand" in the name! Which I assumed was in tribute to Charles Maurice de Talleyrand, the revolutionary French firebrand and sailing enthusiast who proposed the metric system to the French National Assembly in 1790. Had they learned nothing from that old Mars mission brought down in flaming failure for exactly that reason? I remember, as a kid, laughing as my father related the catastrophe, and now the memory haunts me. Could impending doom be my karmic retribution? I wouldn't put that kind of pettiness past the universe.

A laborer informs me the Machine will be operational by "lunchtime", which is not a time. I sigh audibly and hope it's received as a deep breath, but as it turns out, no one is thinking about my breathing.

14:32

"It's ready!" a laborer announces, rushing into the cafeteria, hardhat in hand, a smile squishing his cheeks into cherubic dimples, and I regret the horrible things I've thought about him. We head to a picture window overlooking the factory floor, the most recent development being a 25-meter tall door built into the reconstructed northern wall. In a perfect world, there would be a big, shiny red button. I'd hover over it. Palm raised. The others gathered around, counting down from 10. Voices getting louder and more enthusiastic with each descending integer. Upon reaching zero, I'd slap the button and hard! A bell would sound – maybe even an alarm, this is serious business after all – and everyone would hollar and shout as the Machine roared to life. But that's not how things work in the real world. So, we wait.

And wait.

I make the familiar mental transition from optimism to disappointment combined with feeling stupid for being optimistic in the first place, and prepare myself for a long night of problem-solving when suddenly it happens:

A mechanical *rumble* assaults my ears as each of the Machine's 532,135 moving parts spring into action at once. Everyone cheers. Coworkers pat me on the back, tell me we did it. Which we did not. Yet. Moments later, my pessimism is rewarded when everything stops. Including the back pats. I knew it was too good to be true! I hear *grinding*. Shit. The others step away. This is not good! Then a resplendent sheet of vivid color pours from the Machine onto a massive roll, the only part not wholly contained within its casing. It is happening! And it's beautiful. More so than Leonardo's Mona Lisa and her snarky smile. More than Michelangelo's David and his frightened penis. More than the mosaics of Rome. Because their colors have faded with time. But those pouring from the Machine shine with fresh vibrancy. Blazing blues, piercing greens and deep reds so rich they border on black.

All around me, colleagues celebrate. "High-five". The back pats return. But in truth, I feel only relief. Since I can remember, well-meaning well-wishers have told me to "stop and smell the roses". But I've never been able to, paranoid that satisfaction might vitiate the anxiety I need for motivation. Still, relief is better than nothing and much better than crushing, crushing disappointment.

Mick approaches, smiling like da Vinci's bitch.

"Penny for your thoughts," he says.

Haha, I get it. Because that's my name. "I'm doing great," I say because I'm a liar.

"You did an amazing job."

No shit. "Thank you," I say.

"Awe, Penny, show a little excitement, why don't you?"

Because it would be my ruin! "I just like to stay level. Even keel. Did you know sailboats have keels?"

"Level my arse, Penny. Because of you, our little company now has a complete – I don't want to say 'monopoly', but between you, me and the fence post, a monopoly – over the global stamp trade. Every time anything is sent from one part of the planet to another, it will be with our stamps! No one else can produce product with the cost-effectiveness we can. Not the Pommies, not the Yanks. All because of your patented artificial intelligence driven decision making tree."

"Thank you," I say and run to the bathroom to vomit. A four-flusher that leaves my stomach feeling like I'd just done an Ian Thorpe level abdominal workout. God, Ian Thorpe's abs were tremendous. He could have "Thorpedoed" me any day.

May 15

10:23
We're halfway through the second quarter, and I couldn't be more pleased. The Machine has operated at 101-102 percent efficiency 100 percent of the time. Orders are through the roof, and whichever of our competitors lacked the foresight to liquidate and shutter their doors prior to our takeover has done so. The Machine is expected to have paid for itself within a year, and there is talk of hefty bonuses, presumably none heftier than mine. Still, I'm not without my concerns. For example, and this cannot possibly be my fault, there's the Machine's mathematically impossible output. I am certain there is nothing wrong with my decision making tree. It's too elegant for mistakes. The "decisions" being really just options presented in descending order of desirability. If one source of lumber, for example, eucalyptus, which is widely available, ceases to become so, the Machine will automatically, and at literally light-speed, turn to the next available source, say bottlebrush. When bottlebrush becomes scarce, it might shift to wattle. It's more complicated than that, but that's the gist, and given the fires still ravaging our country, I think goes a long way to explaining our success.

13:58

I enter the boardroom for our half-quarterly all-hands-on-deck meeting two minutes early and take my normal place at the corner near Mick's spot at the head. A few executives are already seated, and I acknowledge them with half-hearted waves, which they return with embarrassing enthusiasm.

Thomas sits down next to me wearing his ridiculous mustard yellow beret. He passes me a folder – it might be old-fashioned, but it's foolproof technology and shows corporate spirit – which I flip through mostly to ensure nothing is missing. For once, there is not.

Mick enters to a chorus of lively salutations, which he soaks in, having none of my aversions to pucker-lipped sycophantry. He flops down on his chair, making it roll two meters backward because he is a man of action. Someone releases a low whistle to signal to the tribe he is part of it.

"Good afternoon!" Mick says in a way that makes everyone think he's talking to *them*. "As you may or may not know, we're on a bit of a roll." Titters. "We've bested the Yanks at their own game!"

"You mean baseball?" says Thomas through a mouthful of chicken breast and pesto panini sandwich that has materialized out of nowhere. I badly want to reprimand him publicly, but everyone laughs, so I join in, making sure my eyes smile too. Thomas' ability to ingratiate himself with the higher-ups through the sheer force of idiocy astounds me. No one else is eating, and why would they? We have literally just returned from a block of time (which, in this case, *is* a time) called lunch. The chicken stink hits my nostrils, and I hold back bile. It smells like Laird and I used to after a weekend of binge drinking and hot sex.

"Just thinking outside the box," says Thomas, and everyone goes, "Ahhh..." Contemplatively! Not adorably, which would be semi-reasonable. It's like he cracked some code, and the expression "thinking outside the box" isn't as thinking inside the box as possible without being inside an actual box.

"You're really something, Thomas. And love the hat!"

"Uh, it's a beret..."

HAHAHAHAHA.

This too shall pass...

Mick continues, wiping a tear. "What I mean is we've got the market cornered Yankee style. We're not a monopoly; I want to make that clear. Our lawyers sure have. We're just the only company left in the space. But enough of that. I want to take this time to congratulate, and I invite you to all join me, our chief engineer, Penny Black."

Everyone applauds except Thomas, who is picking a striation of chicken meat from his teeth with a mechanical pencil.

"Penny has not only got the Machine up and running, but it's working better than we could have dreamed. Over 100 percent." Someone starts applauding, but no one joins in, and they are ruined. Mick shoots me his trademark impossibly symmetrical smile. "Why don't you say a few words, let everyone know how you pulled off this little miracle?"

Shit shit shit shit SHIT SHIT SHIT. "Well, I guess it helps I'm not that good at math," I say. No one laughs. Seriously? Do they really think I think I'm not good at math? Impossible. It must have been my delivery. And after chortling their assess off at the comedic stylings of Thomas no less. "Actually, I'm quite good at math. But even better, I think, at things like logistics and cost-benefit analyses. Which is what the Machine is really about." I shuffle my folder. "For example, most of our stamps have traditionally been made from eucalyptus pulp, but with all the fires-"

Then all hell breaks loose. An alarm, actually many alarms, blare from everyone's cell phones. I check mine:

EMERGENCY ALERT

Suspected series of child abductions.
Scope: Nationwide.
Victim(s): Various.
Suspect(s): None.
Last seen: Nationwide.

"Alright, everyone, settle down. This has nothing to do with us," Mick says, his nerves forged in the fires of boardroom battle and at least one shark attack. "I'm sure everything's going to be fine. False alarm, probably. Happens all the time. I actually know the geezer who came up with the system and to be honest, he's a bogon. Let's just put away our cellies and carry on, right?"

So we do, though I am concerned how much he just let his ocker slang and accent poke through his businessman facade.

16:02

The meeting over, we file out into the cafeteria, the amber alert forgotten by all, it seems, but me. It's not that I particularly care for children. As individuals, they're fine, aside from their complete lack of survival instincts. You'd think it would be obvious even at a young age that roads are not sidewalks and cars are dangerous. But collectively, I see no reason why the government should bankroll an education system that, for all its bells and whistles, still consistently produces output like Thomas.

I head over to the picture window overlooking the Machine and the laborers attending to it. It's mesmerizing. Like a shadow with weight. I check the time. The shift change is in one hour. I try not to dwell on the unsettling feeling welling up inside me, which only makes me dwell on it more.

16:22

Thomas asks if I'd like an espresso, and I make hard eye contact and say I want two, steering into his prejudice and daring him to judge me.

17:01

I casually make my way down to the floor, unnoticed during the always hectic shift change. Outside, visible through the open northern door, are a procession of rail cars lined up as far as the eye can see, waiting to deposit their pulps, dyes and adhesives into the enormous funnel feeding the Machine's inner mechanisms. A handful of engineers (the train kind) mill about waiting to unload their cargo. Starting to feel foolish for getting worked up over nothing, I decide to head home. Except, for reasons I can't quite explain, I pause and unpeel a single stamp. Ned Kelly in full armor. I affix it to the back of my phone and rush for the exit.

18:34

Piloting my ute through Sydney's sprawling suburbs, I cannot shake my building anxiety – really my only constant companion in life. It was particularly bad during my twenties when I had a series of mini-panic attacks culminating in a full-on banger at the dog races one Valentine's Day. Since then, every slight rise in heart rate portends a replay of that horrible night spent face down on concrete surrounded by losing tickets, the voices around me echoing as if filtered through water, whispering in my ear that I'm going to die.

"Screw this," I mutter and pull hard on the wheel. The tires squeal like one of Thomas' chicken farts. There's someone I desperately need to see.

I don't want to.

But I must.

19:07

I pull into Laird's driveway, hoping he isn't home, but I can tell by the light shining through the living room window he is. Laird is not one to waste energy. I mentally rehearse what I'm going to say, but every time, the conversation goes worse. Maybe he'll greet me saying, "Penny! Oh wow! How long has it been?" Or he'll call the police and have me committed for whatever they're calling insanity these days. Is that even possible? It seems like an extreme and arbitrary power to bestow upon private citizens, but it's not like I have an encyclopedic knowledge of psychiatric law. Is that even a kind of law? I shift my Holden into reverse, but before I can hit the petrol, the front door opens, and Laird emerges, waving a friendly wave.

I turn off the engine and exit in a way I hope projects mental stability.

19:09

"Penny! Good to see you," says Laird. So far, so good. We didn't part on the best terms. It wasn't just the rampant infidelity on both our parts or the joint chequing account that devolved into a prisoner's dilemma of preposterous expenditure. We were too different as scientists. As an engineer, my worldview is critical. I look at things like bridges, faucets and escalators and wonder how they can work better. But Laird, being an arborist, who insists on being called an arboriculturist, but don't get me started on *that*, sees the world as something to be coddled and preserved, with the role of scientist being that of steward.

"Laird, I need your help. I think I might be in trouble."

His expression turns dour, and he scrunches his left eyebrow, the right side of his face having been paralyzed during botched childhood ear surgery. "What's wrong, babe?"

He says "babe" platonically, but it's still nice. Makes me think back to when we'd sit on the beach, hold hands, watch drunken Pommy's fall off their rented surfboards, then go for drinks at a nice beach hotel.

"I think I'm responsible for the disappearance and maybe deaths of several children. Maybe dozens. Or hundreds. Or more," I say, finally spitting out what's been eating at me.

He chuckles without humor as if willing it all to be a joke, but my expression and worm-on-the-sidewalk-escaping-rain complexion make clear it is not.

"Why don't you sit down?" he says.

"I don't want to sit down," I reply, sitting down, burying my face in my hands, sucking in deep breaths, trying not to pass out or cry. I haven't shed a tear since Cadel Evans won the 2011 Tour de France, extricating the sport from the Yankee Drug Era, and I don't plan on breaking the streak over something so pedestrian as a complete mental breakdown.

He sits down beside me, puts a, yes, platonic arm around my shoulders. I can tell he doesn't believe me but seems only slightly less disturbed than if he did. "What's going on? You can tell me. I'm sure you're not responsible for, you know, like you said, the deaths of heaps of children. Or adults. Adult humans, anyway..."

"Not the koalas again!" I explode, knowing damn well where this is going.

"Okay, okay. It's just when you destroy an animal's habitat-"

My eyes blaze him into silence. "You know what? Take a look at this," I say and hand him my phone. He looks at it, confused. "Sorry. Turn it over."

He does, and his eyes betray he's clocked the stamp. "Is this-"

"Yes. Evidence of murder."

"No. Ned Kelly. Cool! With the armor and everything."

"And murder! Laird, I'm serious. I'm done. Even if they don't bring back the rope, which they might, just for me. 'Killer Penny' or 'Crazy Penny'. You know, every serial killer's gotta have a nickname."

"Yeah. Um..." He attentively unpeels the strongly affixed stamp and looks it over. Pulls a magnifying glass from between two couch cushions, regards it closer still, his eye appearing gigantic through the glass. It would be comical under less grim circumstances. He takes his time, scanning for details I'd never notice, let alone comprehend. My fingernails dig little blood moons into my palms.

Finally: "This is a normal stamp, Penny. Again, cool picture of Ned Kelly, but other than that, I don't see the problem. Unless you've been packing up kids and mailing them, and they run out of food or something?"

"We would never do that! Ever. Dear lord!"

"I was joking, Penny."

"Oh. Haha?"

"Penny, I'm serious. You-"

"A microscope!" I shout, springing to my feet and banging my shin on the coffee table. Swallow the pain, Penny. *Swallow it.* "You have to look at it under a microscope."

"Why? What is it about this thing that makes you think it's anything other than just a stamp?"

"Just hear me out. My Machine is working at over 100 percent capacity. Maybe that kind of math flies in Treeland, but in my game, there's no remainders. No rounding up. There's two things. Right numbers and wrong numbers, and mine are wrong. Which is where the kids come in. They're free, basically. No receipts. *Kidnapping,* it's called."

"Fine!" Laird says, a mix of pity and horror on his face. "Just give me half an hour; I'll tell you exactly what's in the paper. Okay?"

"Thank you."

"Just you have to promise. If I do this, and there's no bits of..." He trails off, and I save him the embarrassment of not remembering the word "children".

"I promise," I say.

"Good."

Laird heads to the basement, and I sit back down. Look around for something to read.

19:39

Laird returns exactly 30 minutes later, which tells me he probably finished in less time, spending the rest wondering how he might inform a former lover they're our nation's most heinous villain, at least, born domestically. I put down the book I'd found, *More Hilarious Dendrochronology Jokes* (Why was the old tree richer than the young tree? It had more rings!) and rise like a TV character about to learn how the operation went. He takes a deep breath, looks me dead in the eye, and says, "It's just a stamp." I wait for him to say "but" followed by something abhorrent, but he does not.

"No kid bits?"

"None."

"Not even-"

"Nothing."

I take the news in slow, like the first sips of water after escaping the outback. "That's what I thought. It's better to make sure, though. Right? Peace of mind. Connect the T's. Dot the I's. I'm rambling."

"It was good to see you, Penny," he says in a way that tells me it wasn't, and I'm being politely dismissed. I head to the door.

"Wait!" he says, and I turn. Expectantly. There might be a shag in this. "Do you want your stamp back?"

"Keep it!" I say, reclaiming the power in our relationship, and I exit, exonerated of my self-diagnosed crimes. I feel invigorated. Like a scrub python had been constricting my ribs and suddenly let go.

Outside, the air is cool and sweet, and I inhale deeply, drinking it in. By the time I reach my ute and hop in the cockpit, I'm feeling something resembling normal. I fire up the engine, reverse out the driveway, turn on the radio, and smile. My favorite song (hell, everyone's favorite song), *Beds are Burning* by Midnight Oil is on. My lips stretch wide into a smile, and I sing along.

April 30

8:45

I pull into the executive parking lot and am struck by the changes. At least half of the old Falcons and Commodores have been replaced by a glimmering fleet of BMWs, Mercedes and even a few of the Apple roadsters people of poor taste seem so fond of. The laborer parking lot remains about the same after the Board determined increasing their pay would unfairly complicate their lives. In just a few short months, we have gone from a mid-level producer to cornering the global market. The bonus which I'd been hoping would cover my mortgage payments has done so and more, and for the first time I can remember, I feel something approximating happiness. Not all the time, just brief shining moments. Like buying fresh prawns instead of frozen without worrying about the payment going through.

I park, exit my Mercedes-Benz G 63 AMG 6x6, and head to the entrance. The sun is shining; it's not too hot. Like the promise of our great nation has finally, after centuries of colonial rule, corrupt governments and rampaging forest fires been realized. I am concerned that children have continued to disappear and at an increasing rate, somewhere between numerical and exponential, but I sleep soundly at night knowing it's not my fault and has nothing to do with me.

9:15

Mick enters my office wearing a new Rolex on his left wrist that does not compliment the Rolex on his right, but that's Mick for you. His hair has been cut and styled into a "faux-hawk", which I tell him is outdated, but he insists is "retro". This is not an argument I feel qualified to engage in, plus it looks fantastic, and now that I think about it, adds an edge to his look that counterbalances the Rolexes perfectly. His expression is hard to read, which is not a good sign. Like when you can't tell how a puppy is feeling.

"Everything okay?" I ask.

"Yeah, Penny, all good. Just something doesn't add up." I knew it. The Other Shoe of Damocles begins its descent. "I don't see how the math works. What with the fires and us making a paper-based product. Supply and demand and all."

"I don't see what the missing kids have to do with our profits!" I yell, my nerves unfurling like fishing line from an old reel.

He looks at me, confused. "I wasn't saying that. What are you talking about? Though that is a bummer, yeah? Like those high school kids going to Schoolies. Never made it."

"Well, good. It's just a drunken shag fest anyway. They're better off."

"They disappeared, Penny. They're gone. They didn't just miss that, they missed everything."

I am suddenly overwhelmed by intrusive thoughts of mortgage and 6x6 payments. Though I am convinced there's no connection between the missing, really misplaced children and my present financial state, you never know how the media will interpret things. "Why don't you relax, Mick? Go for a surf, maybe. Take a break."

"That's a good idea," he says, forcing a smile, his eyes betraying memories of sharks as I knew they would. He exits my office, shuts the door.

I check my phone and wistfully scroll through old pictures of Laird's dick.

May 15

16:54

These are dark times for our nation, but not us. The fires are out of control, engulfing more than half our great forests. The koala casualties are astronomical, though this receives scant media attention, which is reasonable given most children are gone too. Logically, you'd assume this would free sufficient funds from our education and health care systems to fight the fires, but the government being the government, this has not happened. The outrage in the foreign media has been predictably clamorous but so far has not impacted our stock price.

I text Thomas, who has not shown up for work in days, likely enjoying the fruits of being a young millionaire, spreading his intellectually compromised seed through our city's whore population. I haven't had Gloria Jeans at all during this time, and though I have been gifted a very expensive espresso machine by the Board, it isn't the same. Still, I make a triple, chug it, and start brewing up another.

16:59

I check my phone. Time for drinks! This being Friday end of day. The espresso machine makes a mechanical throat-clearing noise indicating my beverage is finished, and I down it.

17:02

The party is already raging. The laborers have responded to their lack of pay increases by consuming gut-busting levels of free booze every Friday. Some, I've heard, have even constructed special stomach bladders in preparation for the weekend. It's not a healthy strategy, but one I understand and endorse since it means I can toss back eight or nine myself. As my mother used to say, it doesn't matter how drunk you get as long as someone's drunker.

Where the hell is Thomas? Truth be told, I've already started looking for a new assistant, but predictably, haven't received a single application. What a useless generation.

Beds are Burning comes on, and everyone starts dancing, drunk or not, having a great time, shouting out the lyrics. I dance a dance I invented called "Elbowing Ghosts". Screaming at the top of my lungs about broken rivers, bloodwood, boiling Holden wrecks, scared cockatoos, paying rent in reasonable proportions, and of course, the age-old question as to how one can sleep while their bed is on fire.

I suspect one cannot.

As I belt out the words, however, I'm not filled with the overwhelming joy that is the natural response to experiencing perfect music. Rather, I feel a creeping sense of dread. Continuing to elbow ghosts, I can't shake the feeling I've missed something.

BANG! The cafeteria door flies open, and there, standing in the threshold, is Laird. He looks like a dog dragged through hell. His face covered in a ratty beard. His eyes red, streaked with a drainage basin of veins, and encrusted with what I read somewhere is actually snot.

"Stop the Machine!" he yells, stumbling into the room, clutching an almost empty bottle of Johnny Walker Blue. "Stop the Machine!" he repeats, louder and phlegmier.

The party probably ruined, I rush to my former (?) lover, snatch the bottle from his hand. Awfully expensive stuff to be pounding in the daytime. "What are you doing here?" I yell/whisper, grabbing his arm, leading him to the door, or if necessary, a window.

"No!" he yells, grabbing the bottle right back. "We have to stop the Machine!"

"Why?"

"Just follow me. I swear it will make sense."

I am about to call security when Mick walks over. Except, he doesn't just walk. He glides.

"Stay back!" Laird rages notwithstanding Mick's saunter. "Stay back and follow me. Just not too close." Wielding his madness like a scimitar, he backs toward the door, turns, and exits.

We wait until he's gone a distance we feel is consistent with his instructions then follow. Headed toward the Machine.

17:04

I enter the factory floor at the group's lead in time to see Laird drain the bottle like it's Bundy and Coke, then smash it defiantly against the ground. It doesn't break, but the loud *clunk*, I imagine, suffices to make whatever point he intended.

My heart is racing, and I draw in deep breaths, trying to control it. I can't shake the feeling that Laird's breakdown and our previous visit might somehow be connected.

"Don't you see what you've done!" Laird shouts, his red eyes tearing, creating a disconcertingly demonic effect. He stumbles over to the Machine, where the stamps emerge, printed on the finest child-free paper our great nation has to offer and rips off a fistful. An elegant set featuring a water tower from what I'm pretty sure is Gulargambone, New South Wales.

His hands shake, forehead swampy with sweat. A low moan escapes him as he stares down at the irrefutably benign paper product in his clutches. "Look at what you've done!" he says, holding up the stamps like a fallen enemy's head. I now see they do, in fact, depict Gulargambone's water tower and not one of the many others decorating our proud rural towns.

"Laird..." I begin, trying to keep it together and not repeat the damn scene from the damn dog races. "Those are just stamps. They're made from trees. Like you said. Just trees."

A sickly grin stretches a gash in his sagebrush beard. "You're right," he says.

"Well, good," I say.

"Except for one thing."

"Dammit!"

Slowly, he turns the stamps around. Slathering on the drama. God, he's drunk. I hold my breath, expecting something repugnant, except...

It's bright white. Just like the back of any sheet of stamps.

"What the hell, Laird?"

He laughs, coughs, laughs harder, slowly, slowly peels off the backing, and my blood runs cold. It can't be possible. Am I on a reboot of the hit series Prank Patrol? I suspect I am not, and despite my revulsion, I move closer. And closer. Until my worst nightmares are confirmed. The shiny white backing shrouded something horrific. Specks of dark red, dare I say, crimson, and black and brown I need no test to tell me is hair. The off-white, of course, is bone. Then I spot a color that fills me with dread deeper than all the others combined:

Mustard yellow.

"Don't you see what you've done?" Laird says in a voice imbued with humanity I don't deserve. Colleagues and laborers stare. Silent. All knowing what's happened, why, and worst of all, whose fault it is. The woman with the brand new 6x6. A lady who can afford her own booze. This makes me think of Laird and his Johnny Walker Blue, and why he'd waste-

BANG! Laird slumps to the ground, half his head missing, a no doubt Yankee manufactured pistol slipping from his grip and clattering onto the floor. I rush over and collapse on his body.

No no no no no no no Laird please no no no no no.

But he is very dead, and with a flash of insight, I realize what went wrong. The adhesive! Of course, how could I have been so blind? Adhesive is made from acacia which comes from wattle. Wattle! The same wood which the Machine, according to my patented artificial intelligence driven decision making tree began ordering once its normal supplies of eucalyptus and bottlebrush had been burned to ash by the fires. Since there was no wattle left for adhesive, the Machine had to improvise, and apparently, children, once processed, are sticky.

A shadow passes over me, which is, unfortunately, not death but Mick wearing an expression of forlorn, which saddens me because I know I've disappointed him. It was my insistence, after all, that my formulas were sound, and though the ultimate call was his, I've not been shy about claiming my due share of credit, which is most of it. And it's almost definitely my fault I insisted on "making hay while the sun shines" and licensing our technology to non-competitor paper manufacturers across the increasingly burning world.

"Well, Penny, ain't that a pisser,'" he says, not even bothering to hide the ocker he is. "Looks like we're in a heap of bother. Don't be whinging though; we'll get it sorted." He flashes me a tight but warm impossibly symmetrical smile, then bolts, sprinting north, disappearing through the tall open doors. I hear sirens. Someone called the authorities, if not many someones. Laird is dead, and I am responsible for that and the deaths of thousands of children.

Soon to be millions.

Then billions.

I try not to second guess my decision to reject a life of surf and feral cat hunting and reflect on how far our species has come. We haven't done bad. We had a good run! And besides, if I hadn't invented the Machine, someone else would have. In fact, it's probably a good thing it was me and not someone living in a more populated area, where *real* damage could have been done. Although, as I mentioned, the technology will soon be everywhere. Ultimately, it takes a village to raise a child and also to turn one into stamp adhesive.

Click. I turn and see a woman about my age aiming a gun at the back of my head. Her eyes are bloodshot. Her cheeks encrusted with dried mascara. And she's wearing one of the ugliest hats I've ever seen.

"Hey, lady! Nice beret. Where'd you get it? The dump or-"

(*static*)

THE GAME (PART 1)

By
Dr. Edgar Martinez

Editor's Note: The following essay/prophecy of doom is divided into two parts. This is to promote readability, but also the pursuit of the same Holy Grail sought by JK Rowling and others, that is, the division of a single narrative into multiple feature film adaptations. For any Hollywood directors reading this, please note, nudity can be tastefully incorporated into the plot, and though the text is mostly apolitical, it can be easily adapted to suit the ideological persuasions of your target audience. For, while science demands both truth and accuracy, as artists, we are beholden only to the former.

June 11, 2029

The view from the helicopter, a luxuriously appointed CH-47 Chinook, is breathtaking. I'm seated in the passenger compartment along with a team of secret service agents, the presidents of the Coastal United States and China – sharing space for the first time in years, recording artist Bon Jovi, and my head developer, the brilliant Peruvian scientist Dr. Kyle Ricci. I fiddle with my AirPods, sipping a

Manhattan, mentally calculating the cost of its ingredients, which knowing the UN, were a pretty penny. Kyle does not drink normally but serenely sips a glass of something golden brown. I'm not sure how he keeps so calm. I can't. Not with The Game about to begin.

Even above the screaming engine and pounding blades, I can hear the 500,000 strong crowd packed into the stadium below, constructed in record time for this historic event. Though "historic" does not begin to describe the paradigm shift I've spawned. The end of war. Forever. Spotlights blaze in all directions casting the neutral-site host city of Toronto, North America, in a rainbow of strategically non-offensive colors. Purple and teal. Green and orange. Nothing that might imply bias toward either side. CUS President Clinton-Trump peers keenly out her window, presumably scanning for any yellow and red combination that might imply favoritism toward China. Chan Kong-sang, the Chinese President, does likewise, presumably on the lookout for the crimson and gold of the CUS flag.

My people-watching session is interrupted by shrill *beeping*, and I am overcome with annoyance, the emotion I tend to experience most frequently and profoundly. Like when a dishwasher-

BOOM! I see the fireball a split-second before I hear it. The "chopper" lurches, angles groundward. I hear *shattering* and clock the unstrapped copilot crash face-first through the windshield, the rush of cold air cutting off his screams. I, too, am pressed forward, but wearing my seat belt, as always, I suffer no similar fate.

For now.

I smell smoke, oil, burning ozone. The surviving pilot struggles to maintain control of the "whirlybird" and I of my bowels. President Clinton-Trump moans in terror. She wants to go home. Perhaps I've underestimated her courage! Then I realize she's singing the chorus of *The John B. Sails*. I am envious and try to think of interesting last words of my own, but I've nothing.

I hear *banging* behind me, which, presently, is where the blades are, and I am certain they've fallen off, rendering the "autogiro" an anvil. Like a cocky baby bird. Like the amusement park ride where you rise and rise, then drop with only a magnetic brake between you and death. But "eggbeaters" don't have magnetic brakes, and I finally let out the scream building inside me the precise moment the engine cuts out, and everyone can hear.

But I don't care. I scream again.

And again.

Until my throat is shredded.

Two Years Earlier

(Editor's Note: In the film adaptation, we can communicate this information via title card).

I am at my desk staring at my computer but not really looking at it. I've written close to a million lines of code yet feel I've barely started. It seems like forever since I quit my job down at Pornhub, where I made a nice living with good benefits but was not fulfilled. To be clear, I wasn't involved in the, shall we say, content creation. I've no taste for smut. There's just only so much work to be done on a website that's already built. There was no satisfaction waiting for problems to arise I could easily solve, notwithstanding the distracting moans of self-flagellating coworkers.

I rise with an involuntary grunt from my Herman Millar Aeron chair, stolen, as all my valuables from P-hub. It cost a fortune to sanitize but still much less than what a Herm' typically goes for even used. The coffee maker, bless its heart, gurgles to completion, only steps away – everything in my office is only steps away – and I roll over, pour a cup. To the brim and even over, thanks to the miracle of surface tension. Science, as the Bon Jovi poster above my desk teaches us, does indeed "rock".

I take a sip, leaning against the photocopier, which was here when I moved in and probably hasn't worked in a decade. Suffice to say, I would never steal a photocopier from P-hub. The coffee is not expensive but is delicious. Strong. No cream, no sugar. Like Juan Valdez intended. My eyes feel heavy despite the psychological jolt offered by the caffeine and I pray I can stay awake until the physical effects kick in.

I hear a *bing* from my computer, take another sip, return to my desk, and flop down on my remarkable feat of ergonomic engineering, made right here in the CUS. With my free hand, I wiggle my non-wireless mouse (batteries have become prohibitively expensive lately), and the screen flashes to life. A lone email resides in my inbox with the subject heading "JOB APPLICATION", sent by one "Dr. Kyle Ricci."

Two days later, I am seated on a bench facing the reflecting pool fronting the Washington Monument, a location I chose specifically for its association with important, secret meetings, and because I can't afford a restaurant and don't want my office to be Dr. Ricci's first impression. Plus, if need be, the spire can provide an easy segue into my past employment. It isn't raining, which is too bad. It would have added to the spy thriller effect I'm going for, but it's cold enough that the area is relatively deserted, so there's that.

"Dr. Martinez?" I hear, and whirl around to see a short man with an expressionless face but kind eyes standing directly behind me *(Editors Note: This could be a jump scare in the movie???)*. It takes me a beat to recover, but I'm able to smoothly downshift into cool and reply:

"Yes."

"I'm Dr. Ricci."

Thank God. I was worried he was some kind of assassin, and not just because he appears to be Peruvian. He sits down and gazes at the faintly rippling water, steel grey like the sky.

"Thank you for coming," I say.

"Thanks for the invite. Hey, is this where they shot *All the President's Men*?"

"Yes," I say because probably.

"That was a great movie."

"Incredible," I say because how does he know I haven't seen it? And I've heard it spoken of plenty of times. "I think, now that you mention it, this is where they did the Smoking Man scenes."

"Wasn't that *The X-Files*?"

"No."

"Yeah, I'm pretty sure you're thinking of Deep Throat."

"The hell I am!" I snap, my mind flooded with filth.

We resume our silent stares. A duck lands with a splash. Ripples ensue.

"So, what's this all about? Your post was fascinating. Truly. But how do I say this? Ending all war forever is, uh, ambitious."

I can't let this fish get away. Not with his education and non-pornographic background. "Do you think you're up for that, though? Saving the world? Which is what we'd be doing, basically. It's just that... I can't help but think of war as, well, embarrassing. I'm embarrassed that, as far as we've come as a species, we're still building weapons for no reason other than to blow people to pieces. Blow children to pieces. They can call smart bombs "smart bombs" and talk about all the humanity that goes into their precision. But there's nothing precise about bombing weddings and funerals and whatever else to maybe prevent some crime somewhere. I just can't help thinking of the children, man! Because every time, that's one more kid who'll never get to go to school. Never get to fall in love. Never get to be cool."

"Isn't that from *Rockin' in the Free World*?"

"I don't have anything to pay you!" I blurt, getting to the point. "But I do believe in what I'm doing and what we can do together. Your resume is extraordinary. A PhD in quantum physics from Cal Tech. Another in computer science from The University of Paris. How is Paris, by the way? I've never been."

"Everything you'd imagine."

"I have to go someday."

"You should."

"Uh, lead developer at Ubisoft. Lead developer at Electronic Arts. And captain of the Pictionary team at all of them."

"Actually, at Cal Tech, I was only co-captain."

"Still, I don't think I've ever seen that great a resume."

"I have," says Kyle.

"Really?" I reply skeptically. "Who's?"

He smiles, his whole face now as affable as his eyes. "Yours," he says.

I smile back.

Two weeks later, we are a well-oiled machine. Like a flock of birds, dipping and darting among the clouds in perfect synchronicity. How are they connected? Probably through the Earth's electromagnetic field, but no one really knows. Kyle is a master of efficiency, and though I was concerned that the office, which is too small for one person, would be much too small for two, he's actually made things more comfortable. Shifting a desk here, throwing out a photocopier there. Stacking mugs instead of displaying them on a Burger King food tray. We buzz around on our Herms', the wheels literally well oiled. And best of all, we're getting things done.

"How's the character creation menu coming?" I ask, sliding to the coffee pot where I fill my sparkling new thermos.

"Great. Almost done. And I think it should meet our needs nicely."

Of course. Mr. Efficiency on the case. "How so?" I ask, sliding back.

His eyes twinkle. "How have we – well, you – been doing it up to now?"

I like how he caught himself there. Shows he's a team player, not just in it for the credit. "Same as with most games. We have a set number of characters and traits but with pretty much unlimited customization options. Why, what have you got brewing in that big head of yours?"

He twirls a few chin hairs. "You know what? Can you just give me a little more time? I want to make sure everything's perfect before I start talking a lot of big talk."

"No problem. I'm looking forward to it when you're done."

"Thank you, sir. What are you working on?"

"Weapons," I say, sighing.

"What's the issue?" he asks, eyebrows rising into an empathetic peak.

"Specificity, man. When I was working on *Half-Life,* we could do whatever we wanted. A gun that shoots saw blades? No problem, fire it up."

"I liked that gun."

"Yeah, it was a big hit, and not *that* many kids lost fingers. But honestly, I don't know what the latest weapons, say, the Australian military is using. I can look it up, but I don't think their top generals are doing Wikipedia entries."

"Who'd want to go to war with Australia?"

"No one! It's just an example. Well, New Zealand maybe because of the whole big brother, little brother thing. You're a sheep fucker, you're a kangaroo fucker..."

"Like Cleveland and Akron."

"Sure."

"I don't think that's gonna be a problem, though."

"How do you figure?"

Kyle doesn't answer, vocally. Instead, he clicks a file, types a very long password, and opens a document containing the full military arsenals of every country on the planet.

"Where did you get this?"

He shoots me a look that says he'd rather not say, and I respect that. God knows we all have our secrets. P-hub's search result data taught me that.

"Can you email that to me?"

"Rather not," he says. Then adds, "But..." Clicks *print.* And the high-efficiency, low-ink printer we've rented starts spitting out pages.

"Great. Thanks, Kyle."

"You're very welcome. Anything else?"

"Not right now. Unless you want to talk about the map real quick?"

"Yeah! Actually, I was thinking we could base it on historical conflicts? I have info on pretty much every war ever dating back to..." He clicks some files. "...the Peloponnesian War."

"Interesting. But I want to keep things neutral. Don't want to give anyone an unfair advantage. Pelopennisians especially. And let's be creative. Have fun with it."

"Sounds like a plan," he says. But his words do not register. Something in my news feed has drawn my attention. I read several articles. It takes only seconds. "Kyle, have you been keeping up with what's happening with the CUS and China?"

"Just there's some kind of trade dispute."

"Looks like it's turning into more than a dispute."

"Oh, really," he says and is almost immediately by my side, taking no longer to read the articles than I did. Maybe less time. Jesus. "Very interesting."

"We're going to need to speed things up," I say.

"I think you're right."

"Easier said than done, though. It would be one thing if, I don't know, we knew someone in Congress. But I don't. And I'm guessing you don't either."

"Hmmm... Let me check," he says, unpockets his phone, holds it up, and casually scrolls through every Member of Congress. Names. Numbers. Emails. Home addresses. Geolocations. It's all there.

"Nice work," I say, leaving it at that.

A month later, I am climbing the steps of the Capitol Building, surrounded by security, mentally rehearsing my speech. The entire House and Senate are expected to attend, and already politicians on all three sides are jostling to both take credit for and decry my work, though it's far from complete. Not that I intend to harp on that particular tidbit of info.

Inside, I am, like everyone entering the building that day regardless of status, strip-searched, hosed down, and issued that day's uniform – an off-the-rack Hugo Boss suit that fits decently and is probably more appropriate than the cargo shorts, comedic T-shirt (Shroedinger's cat walks into a bar. And doesn't!) and tweed blazer I'd worn hoping to play up the whole "eccentric genius" angle.

The Chamber of the House of Representatives is even more impressive than advertised. Like a Greek amphitheater chiseled from wood and preserved with Lemon Pledge. Until now, I've seen it only while bingeing presidential State of the Union addresses, which *tend* to focus on policies that are, shall we say, contrary to mine, but, still, I learned a great deal about how to sell them in the process.

I am ushered to the podium. The President herself is front row center, surrounded by her husband, parents and in-laws. I am surprised to see them and not just because of the well-documented inter-family tensions. The event already had a huge target on it, and now it's got a bigger one. What I'm proposing – we're proposing – could completely upset the defense spending apple cart, and a lot of the apple merchants are angry. They have apple tree payments to make. And their constituents are angry too, convinced by the apple merchants that paying for apple cart paths and picking machines is crucial if they want to work at the apple juice factory that doesn't exist.

I pump my fist in celebration of my metaphor, but there's no time for smelling roses. I have a speech to make and can't be distracted. Not by my burgeoning stage-fright. Not my pithy inner monologue. And definitely not the fact nobody else's hair seems quite as wet as mine.

I reach into my pocket where my speech is not because this is not my suit.

Dammit. Stay calm, Edgar. You can handle this. Mrs. Martinez didn't raise no fools. "Thank you," I begin. That's not what I wrote, though! What did I? "Hello...?" That's it! Thank God. It all starts coming back. "Folks, I stand before you today to present an opportunity that could change humanity forever. Until now, we have fought wars with violence, dating back to our days as tribal primates."About a third of the room goes ice cold. "If you believe that sort of thing. You know, *evolution*." I say "evolution" with a stinky face, and this appeases them. I continue. "But I ask myself, why? Why not instead choose discussion? Compromise. Because isn't that how all wars end anyway? With a treaty or agreement? So why not cut out the middleman – the war itself?" A hell of a lot more than a third of the room goes ice cold. "Stay with me, folks. I'm not finished! At the same time, there has to be some value in conflict, right? Otherwise, we wouldn't do it." A few heads nod. "The question then becomes, how do we avoid the horrors of war while still keeping the... How do I say this? *Advantages*." All eyes are on me. I take a deep breath. The words of our greatest presidents echoing through my mind:

"The fiery trial through which we pass will light us down in honor or dishonor to the latest generation..." Honest Abe.

"In the future days, which we seek to make secure, we look forward to a world founded upon essential human freedoms..." Franky D.

"It's morning in America..." The Gipper. Ronny R. The man who mastered the pitch and to whom I owe an incomprehensible creative debt.

Finally, I exhale and spit out the words I've rehearsed over and over with Kyle, a perfect encapsulation of how I intend to end all war everywhere and forever:

"*Let's game it out...*"

I arrive at the office to find Kyle standing on his desk, hanging a framed copy of today's *Washington Post* front page, at least a print-out of their website's homepage, featuring my quote and a headshot from my film extra days. He hops down and embraces me warmly. "You did it, buddy. You did it. They were eating out of your hand. You called them 'folks'. You nailed the line. You were on fire."

"I don't know. I almost lost them for a second there with the whole evolution thing."

"Yeah, what happened? I thought we took that out?"

"Long story. Security was nuts."

"Security added the line?"

"Anyway, yeah," I say, stretching. "It went great. I think we're going to get that contract. It's happening, buddy! And I'm telling you, if those fat cats in the military-industrial complex don't like it, they can kiss my hairy-"

BOOM! An explosion rips through the office, and everything goes black.

I awake in a much too bright room with Kyle standing over me along with a number of military types whose uniforms indicate high rank.

"Morning, sleepy-head," says Kyle, knowing, as always, the right thing to say.

"Morning, sleepy-head," I say and instantly regret it the same way I do telling someone "Happy birthday" on my birthday when it is not their birthday, and they just said it to me. "Where am I?"

"You're in the Pentagon, buddy."

"Not a hospital?" I say, noting I am in a bed and there are machines hooked up to me.

"It's a hospital in the Pentagon."

I look around. "It seems a lot like an office."

"It is. But also a hospital since you're a patient and in it."

"Okay," I say, conceding whatever the point is.

"You'll be working here from now on," says a tall woman whose face is mostly cheekbones. I guess she's in charge. "The explosion may have just been a warning, but we can't risk it."

"How's an explosion a 'warning'? Seems a little excessive. Kyle, we talked about this. Tell her!"

She glares at him with almost pigmentless eyes, and he's quieted. "We're dealing with excessive people," she says.

"What? Too many people? And when did it get so foggy in here?"

"Get this man some coffee; I think he's concussed," says Cheekbones, heading to the door. The green suits follow and exit, leaving Kyle and me alone.

"Did she just say...?"

"Well, bud, it's not foggy."

"What are we doing here? What's going on?" I ask, my brain clenching like a dehydrated monkey fist.

Kyle tells me. And holy shit.

Since I've been comatose, hostilities between the CUS and China have intensified. The trade dispute, it turns out, revealed profound and ultimately irreconcilable differences, ideologically speaking, between the two nations. Understanding how requires a brief look at some recent history as it has been explained to me by Kyle, thus all errors are his.

Chinese President Chan Kong-sang came to power promising to usher in a new age of prosperity. A "Golden Age", as he called it. And he delivered. Sweeping measures were implemented promoting worker rights, fair wages, safety standards and other policies consistent with the original tenants of communism as articulated by Marx and others. There was considerable backlash among the nation's well-heeled and political elites, but they could do relative squat given the president's soaring approval rating and myriad accomplishments, including making the Chinese national basketball team internationally competitive.

The CUS, meanwhile, was experiencing something of a "Renaissance", as President Clinton-Trump called it. She had been elected in a landslide on a platform consistent with the original tenants of free-market capitalism as articulated by Smith and others. Slashing red tape and taxes. Only three percent of voters supported her challengers, a school teacher and human rights activist from Maine and a pylon that gained low-key fame as an improvised plot devise in the hit Taylor Lautner vehicle *We're All Outta Megaphones!* She promised to send the nation's GDP "skyrocketing" and to "ramp up the average wage", and like her counterpart, she delivered.

The problem was, while each set of policies worked in a vacuum, they ultimately mixed like oil and water, which were also part of the dispute but not the main problem. That would be the price of goods. With Chinese workers enjoying CUS-level rights, the cheap goods Camericans depended on became prohibitively expensive. Clothing quadrupled in price. Manufactured goods like spatulas, frying pans and mixing bowls went up tenfold. And anyone not of means who wanted to purchase a cell phone had to first secure a "Hello Friends Mortgage". Most economic models predicted the "skyrocketing" GDP and "ramped up average wage" would mitigate these costs; however, they failed to account for how wildly a few newly minted trillionaires would skew such macro-level data. Most people, it turned out, lacked the means even to make pancakes.

China was not faring much better. With less demand for its goods, work became scarce, and black markets quickly emerged where worker rights were perhaps even more scarce than before. With full-scale depressions immanent, and leaders inexorably divided along ideological lines, there was, unfortunately but not unsurprisingly, a growing appetite for war. Worst of all for Kyle and me were rumors the dispute might be resolved not by armed conflict but a seven-game, winner-take-all basketball tournament between the CUS and China, whose teams ranked one and two worldwide, with both sides claiming, not unreasonably, that their team was the most talented. Had the best chemistry. The tallest players. And the idea was gaining traction.

"They'll never do it," says Kyle, having brought me up to speed.

"But say they do."

"They won't! No one cares about sports."

"No! *We* don't care about sports. For everyone else, they're quite popular."

"Not people under 40."

"I don't know..."

"Okay. Remember the game we researched last night at the *Sow n' Cow*?"

"Yeah. I remember. I got pancakes and you were jealous because you got that shitty fishburger and you're still thinking about it. I was wondering what the hell pancakes had to do with-"

"*Anyway.* Last night's game. The clock is ticking down. A guy takes a shot, misses. Buzzer goes off. They lose. Game over. And you know what happened to him?"

"Nothing. His teammates actually seemed quite supportive."

"Exactly. They didn't even shoot him. He probably just went home to his family or something. How is that good in any way?"

"It isn't."

"Exactly. No headshots. No blood. Just a bunch of gangly weirdos running around. And did you see the uniforms? Who wears teal these days?"

"No one! The retro-90s were a long time ago."

"Exactly!" Kyle says, contemplatively twirling a few chin hairs, then muses, "Maybe, and I'm just throwing this out there, but maybe we can, I don't know, get rid of them somehow?"

“Huh. There’s a thought,” I reply, twirling a few chinnies of my own, evaluating his seriousness. He seems serious. So I say, “What do you propose? Hypothetically.”

“Well,” he says. “Have you ever, and again, I’m just putting this out there, but...”

“Relax, man. We’re just spitballing.”

“Okay,” he says, lips curling into a smile. “Have you ever, hypothetically, hacked a Twitter account?”

The next few weeks fly by in a blur of programming, negotiating, and occasionally, eating and sleeping. We lost everything in the explosion; however, this freed us to start over without all the glitches and quirks that had been woven into the programming fabric through constant revisions and tinkering. Parts of the map that had once been rife with unnecessary warp zones and pneumatic tubes are now clutter-free. Weapons that had once only superficially resembled the real thing are now virtually indistinguishable. Kyle is a machine during this time, rarely leaving his workstation, sleeping in the office most nights curled up on a cot provided at exorbitant cost by the government. I’ve all but given up trying to keep up with him, but that’s what makes us a great team. I don’t have to.

As for me, my focus is on the business side of things. If my bosses are going to take my proposal to their bosses, and those bosses have no bosses, they need to know they can sell it. I check my phone. It’s time to go. “Alright, I’m off!” I say, waking Kyle.

“All set?” he asks sleepily, peeling his face from his mechanical keyboard.

“As all set as I’ll ever be.”

He gives me a thumbs-up, which is an old-timey symbol for "erection", but I don't tell him. Just let him drift back to Dreamland.

My dress shoes (I don't know what brand, but they are dark brown) *click* loudly as I head down a spartan hall, cleared out of "an abundance of caution" I might trip and fall on something, which I find preposterous. Yes, I've been tripping and falling a lot lately, since the concussion, but I still find the measure excessive, insulting and just adds to the gaggle of nerves roosting in my gut.

Click click click click click click click.

Click click click click click click click.

I arrive at an ancient oak door with crimson and gold CUS flags displayed on each side and knock.

"Come in," says a familiar, highly resonant voice.

I enter and close the heavy door behind me. General Cheekbones, or whatever her name is, rises from a magnificent antique chair. More a throne, really. The towering, carved mahogany back is adorned with golden vines twisting around forest green padding stuffed, no doubt, with horsehair. It must be a meter and a half tall, not counting the twin knobs carved into pinecones. I think of my Herm with disgust. Comparison is not the thief of joy but rather a magician who reveals its absence. "Thanks for coming," she says. "Have a seat."

"Thank you," I say, grateful she did not address me by name and settle into the second most impressive chair I've seen today.

She starts at me immediately. "This is big. Really big. Big swing, your proposal. But frankly, I'm not sure what to think. It sounds great. But I'm not sure what to think."

"I think it's fantastic."

She stares at me twirling a black Bic between her disconcertingly long fingers, a detail I notice since that's my go-to analog writing instrument and always has been. Thank God I stocked up while they were affordable. "Look, nobody cares about basketball," I say, approaching the point.

"That's true. Disgusting what they tweeted about those orphans. And to them. And what was with the puppets? What kind of sicko would even think that?"

"The most disgusting of the disgusting of the disgusting."

"Exactly. Someone should cut off their-"

"Right! As I was saying, because of that, the basketball player thing, and since no one wants a nuclear war, I think we should... *game it out.*"

"I do like the ring of that."

Of course, she does. "Exactly. We combine the hottest thing in popular culture for the kids with non-mutually assured destruction for the kids at heart."

"Okay. Okay. But how do I sell that?"

"Let's game it out!"

"I got that. What I'm... Hey, isn't that what you just said?"

"Yeah."

"You're manipulating me!"

"Yeah!"

She stares at me for a long time. If life was a cartoon, I would be getting smaller and she larger. "Impressive," she says finally. "I think we might be on to something here. Great work. Great pitch."

She rises, and we shake hands. My hand has never felt smaller, and I have never felt so alive. I turn and almost collide with a man about my size who has just entered the office.

"Excuse me," I say.

"Sorry, I didn't think you'd still be here."

"No problem. Have we met?"

"No. I've never seen you before, and I don't know who you are."

"Well, you have yourself a good day," I say, on top of the world. He seems like an odd duck, but what the heck. I like his style. His blazer, in particular, reminds me of one I myself once owned. It says I might be dressed up, but I'm still a fun guy, and my favorite season is probably autumn. But it's not autumn now; no, spring is in the air if not on the calendar. It's a brand new day, and Kyle and I are about to grab it tenderly by the balls.

THE GAME (PART TWO)

By
Dr. Edgar Martinez

Editor's Note: Since the preceding represents the narrative's approximate halfway point, it may be prudent for anyone producing the live-action adaptation to start the second film here. To this end, I propose punching up the above"ending". A conveniently timed explosion may do the trick, which is always a fun plot device and has occurred just once thus far. And wasn't that a thrilling moment! Also, the film adaptation should be gritty. Think Nolan's Batman.

We have been working for the last 48 hours straight, Kyle and I, except for the odd microsleep. I swear I've slept more on long drives. Speaking of which, we have taken to wearing headbands designed for long-haul truckers that shoot jolts of electricity through our skulls if our heads tilt down past a certain angle. It's an effective way to stay awake and well worth the switch to slip-on shoes.

Despite our physical fatigue, our minds remain relatively sharp. We've been working so long and hard another few days are just another drop in the metaphorical rag. Plus, we'll sleep plenty a few days hence.

"I think we're ready to create ourselves a character and do a little map tour," Kyle says.

"Really? You're not messing with me?" I say, enjoying a rare shot of natural adrenaline.

"No, sir."

I roll over to his workstation, and he clicks a few keys. The letters have long been typed off. The screen takes a few seconds to load, and my mind is assaulted by disaster scenarios, then it flashes to life, and I can breathe again. There are three featureless digital humanoids floating in a cyan blue void.

"Here's our competitors. Let's call them 'Team A'," he says. *Click click click.* Two humanoids disappear, leaving one plus dozens of slideable scales representing attributes like strength, constitution, aim, aggression, dexterity, patience, dependability, courage and many, many more. "Here's our first guy, and, just for fun, let's say he's you."

"Okay," I reply, a bit nervous. "Do you have a face that looks like mine?" I say *mine* like it would be prejudicial if he didn't.

"Don't need one."

"What? How?"

"I'll show you." *Click click click,* and dozens of images of yours truly appear on screen via the internet. He clicks on one of me at my birthday dinner at the *C n' S*, humorously "drinking" a bottle of cream soda through a french fry "straw". Moments later, my face is on the avatar minus the hilarity.

It's terrifying. "Fascinating!" I say.

"Now, the best part. It's based on a game I once did called *Friend Fight.* The idea was it's a fighting game, but it's you versus your friends based on your actual physical attributes and skills. It promoted fitness so was not popular, but I'm thinking it's perfect for us. I would have shown you before, but I wanted to be sure I got it right."

"Fascinating!"

"So, let's do this!" he says, beaming. "How many push-ups can you do?"

"About 50."

"Really?" Kyle says, looking me over. "Because there is testing before the actual competition. You can't just-"

"At least 50. Probably a hundred by now. But say 50 to be safe."

"Okay." *Click click click.* The avatar's muscle mass increases. Skin tightens. Vascularity improves. Attributes like strength and power increase. Others, meanwhile, decrease. Like endurance, which makes no sense. As an old steeplechaser, I should know.

"Vision?"

"Twenty-twenty," I say, playing around with a contact lens trying to emigrate inside my head.

Click click click, and aim improves.

About a half-hour later, my avatar is complete, and a few hours after that, we have completely explored the map, and it is flawless. Not just flawless, perfect. The animation isn't just beautiful; it's ideally beautiful. Suitable for all ages and oh-so adaptable into merch. And while there is still work to be done incorporating actual gameplay, we're close enough, in my estimation, to conclude, more or less, we've done it.

We've done it!

I text "Cheekbones" and type, "Hey we're ready." I then delete "Hey" and cheekily press *send* without capitalizing the "w". Seconds later, my phone *dings*. I look down, scream in pain, then bring the device to eye level. She has replied with a thumbs up.

It's go time.

My nerves aren't shot, but they're getting there. Just 24 hours until what the media has dubbed, as strongly prompted, "The Game". While our work is technically completed, we're expected to play a ceremonial role. So, the brass has determined it would be good publicity for me and Kyle, now wearing a tight-fitting metal collar flashing a friendly green light around his neck, to meet the CUS team for a photo opportunity. Thus, we are traveling via bulletproof stretch Maybach to their training center located somewhere in the local professional football team's stadium. The streets are empty, but it doesn't feel like it. More like our limo is surrounded by cheering ghosts.

We approach our destination, pass through a series of gates, and the engine roars as the driver accelerates toward a very solid-looking stadium wall. I brace for impact, but a hidden door slides open, and we are in a tunnel lit by long halogens spaced at intervals that create a 1980s, inter-dimensional CGI effect.

"Have we done the right thing?" Kyle asks.

"Of course!" I say, chuckling. "Tomorrow is a big day and not just for us and our bank accounts. We're helping civilization emerge from its primordial ooze of violence-"

"You're just quoting the press release."

"Which we wrote together," I say, leaning back in the buttery rich alpaca leather seat. "Don't worry about it. Relax."

The limo slows then rolls to a stop, just as I'm getting comfortable, and my door is wrenched open by a burly soldier sporting full tactical gear and a metal collar around his neck just like Kyle's.

"You guys are twins," I joke, though Kyle does not hear me.

We are escorted through a series of drab concrete hallways, eventually reaching an air-sealed vault, where we are scanned for weapons and transmissible diseases, then sprayed with disinfecting mist that smells like lilacs. A *beep* sounds, a heavy door swings open, and I find myself face-to-face with Cheekbones.

"Hello, General Kirkpatrick," says Kyle.

General Kirkpatrick! "General Kirkpatrick," I say, "great to see you again."

"Gentlemen," she says, turns, and we follow her down yet another concrete hallway, this one a lighter grey, shinier, and which slopes noticeably downward, engaging in a classic Washington walk-and-talk. "The team is ready. At least, as ready as they can be. We're asking a lot of them, as you know. But we did our due diligence. Auditioned over 10 million candidates, ages ranging from seven to 42."

I whistle when I hear "42".

"None of the 42-year-olds qualified," she says, and I whistle again, this time relieved. "They're the best of the best. Champions all. Reflexes: off the charts. Intelligence: off the charts. Physical fitness: pretty good, actually. Of course, the enemy squad is no doubt just as talented, probably more so."

"Uh..." Kyle mutters, gripping his neck collar.

"Don't worry, Dr. Ricci. It's a numbers thing. They have more options to choose from."

"Then how can we win?"

"Simple," she says. "Teamwork."

"But won't they have teamwork too? I mean, aren't they communists? Isn't that kinda their thing?"

Before she can answer, we reach a towering door, likely titanium, guarded by yet another fearsome soldier. She presses a button, it slowly swings open, and we enter the largest room, if you can even call it that, I've ever seen. It must be twice the size of the stadium above and is divided roughly into two sections. The first is bank upon bank of softly glowing, jet black servers, like a sleeping robot army that causes local rolling brownouts. The second is for training. This includes state-of-the-art fitness equipment, strategically non-state-of-the-art fitness equipment, massage tables, hot tubs, cold tubs, a meditation waterfall, and, at the absolute center of it all, the main gaming stage. Built identically to that they'll compete on. Stretching 20 meters skyward, like a carbon fiber fortress of solitude, with giant screens and speakers jutting out at seemingly random but visually and auditorily perfect angles. At the base are three highly customized gaming setups, their main feature being 3D treadmills that, in addition to facilitating unfettered horizontal movement, also rise and fall vertically via thousands of electrically charged high tensile steel pins. Occupying this technological menagerie is our team in the flesh, resplendent in full-body haptic feedback and motion capture VR suits and headsets, all, of course, crimson and gold. A physical bell, like the kind they use in boxing, *rings.* They disengage from their setups, remove their headsets, taking care not to interfere with their blinking neck collars, and jog over, wiping sweat from their brows with single-use towels that are instantly collected by someone whom I suspect it's their only job.

General Kirkpatrick makes the introductions. "Team, I'd like you to meet the men who made all this possible."

"Men and women," I correct her.

"Were women involved?"

"No."

We solemnly bump elbows with our team, the moment's significance lost on no one, and I make sure this is reflected in my countenance. I can't believe how young they all look. Because they are young! Jesus. Has anything changed? Are we any more civilized than the barbarians who sent children just like these to die in the deserts of Iraq, jungles of Vietnam and trenches of Europe? I still think "yes", but it's a softening "yes".

General "Cheekbones" Kirkpatrick approaches a tall but rail-thin boy who can't be older than 13 and puts her hands on his shoulders, enveloping them. "This is Lee, better known as 'ToTLee'."

"He's wearing glasses!" I blurt, suddenly unconcerned with social norms pertaining to sightedness.

"They're just for the look. I'm going for a nerdy kinda thing," he says, trying to quell my fears, but his cracking voice does anything but. It's too bad they're testing for steroids and whatever else we pump our best traditional athletes full of till their bones change.

The General continues, "Lee is our marksman. The best shot in the country. Maybe the world. He won the *Fortnite* World Cup in singles and duos the last two years. He's a master of *Call of Duty*, *Storm of Valor*, *Tapeworm Simulator*, you name it. Best of all, he's got a dozen major sponsorships from all over the world. And don't be fooled by his physique," she says, shaking him like a wet noodle. "Lee has the endurance of a sled dog. What's your fastest 10k time again?"

"Twenty-nine minutes flat," he says, which does sound pretty fast. I do some quick math based on my steeplechase times. It's actually *really* fast.

"Up next is Maria AKA 'ButrFethRz'. She's here for strategy. Not only is she a gaming superstar, she graduated from Cornell with a PhD in military tactics and strategy. She's one of those savant kids. Breezed through high school in nine weeks blah blah blah. And she's got, count 'em, 19 major sponsorships. Or is it 20 now?"

"Um, it's 20," she says. "But seriously, can we talk about The Game? We have a lot-"

"She doesn't look particularly athletic," I say, suddenly unconcerned with social norms pertaining to anything.

"I play darts, billiards and foosball," she claps back. "I'm very coordinated."

"Perfect!" I say because I want to keep my job.

"Finally, there's Britney AKA LaZrFace," she says, approaching a girl, about 10, whose eyes radiate a predatory intelligence that makes me glad she's on our side. "Our team leader. LaZrFAce can do it all. The most well-rounded gamer we've got with, let's just cut to the chase, how many sponsorships now?"

"Is that all really a priority?" Kyle butts in.

"Of course not, but don't tell our sponsors," the General says to scattered laughter.

Kyle furrows his brow. "But-"

"Picture time!" someone shouts, and we gather like the old friends I'm sure we'll someday be. We smile, say "Cheese", get the shot, and it's time to go.

"Great to meet you all," I say. "We're counting on you. And I know you'll do great."

They mumble thanks as children do. We bump elbows good-bye and are escorted to the exit as the team returns to their stations. Again, we find ourselves walking and talking. I look to Kyle. "What do you think? A pretty impressive group, I thought."

"I guess."

"What do you mean, 'I guess'?"

"Nothing. There's nothing we can do. *Now*. So why worry?"

I stop walking, grab Kyle by the arm. "I gotta tell you, man, this pissy new attitude isn't working for me. What is it? Because of this?" I say, taping his collar, and he recoils in horror.

"No! This thing? No. I mean, what are the odds-"

"Fifty-fifty."

"Right. Fifty-fifty. Seems like an artificially round number."

"It's what the algorithm came up with. And given both sides are nuclear powers, it could have been a lot worse."

"I guess."

"Come on! It'll be fine. The team looks great. Did you see how many sponsorships they have?"

"I did. It's just hard to judge someone by that and looking at them."

"They can't lose. I promise."

"How can you possibly think that?"

"It would be devastating for the economy. I think the algorithm calculated a 10 trillion-dollar penalty for the loser. Speaking of artificially round numbers."

"I'm talking about having my head blown off my shoulders!" he shouts, clutching his collar.

"Oh, come on! Think how much worse it would be if we had the actual war and you died however you were probably going to die anyway. I've heard radiation poisoning is the worst way to go. Your hair falls out. Your eyes turn into, like, prunes. Just shrivel up, nothing you can do."

"How do you know I would have been one of the 135 million people, exactly, apparently, to die? That's just odds based on a simulation."

"Actually billions of simulations, so..."

"The whole thing is absurd."

"Don't say that," I say, genuinely hurt. "We all had the same odds of getting a collar."

"Oh right, yeah. The Lottery. Don't tell me that wasn't rigged."

"How could they have? It was based on social insurance numbers. Drawn randomly."

"Then why don't any of the brass have them?"

"They might have pulled a few strings, but for a reason. Even if we eliminate actual wars, we still need people – experts in the field – to decide whether to have digital ones. Conflict doesn't stop just because war has."

He takes a breath as if to reply, then just exhales.

"What?"

"Nothing."

"What?"

"Why don't you have one?"

"A what?"

"A collar!"

"Oh! Odds, man. Do I need to get you a calculator? There's two of us-"

"I get it. But don't you think this could have worked fine without the loser still having to suffer the same consequences as actually going to war?"

"We talked about this. Then everyone would wage simulated war all the time. It would lose the impact. We'd go right back to regular wars with the same casualties plus all the damage and destruction you usually get. Now there's none. Just the losing side has to pay for whatever it would have cost anyway. This is a better system, period."

"I would have at least liked to have had a fighting chance."

"You do! Those kids are your fighting chance. Now, Kyle, I need to know you're with me on this. Are you?"

He takes a deep breath, exhales, and with the last of his air, whispers, "Yes."

Today is The Day! The whole world is watching or will be in a few hours. Even the sternest owner of the stankest coal mine is giving their employees the day off. Because, whatever happens, tomorrow will be different. Whichever country wins, not only will their economy be infused with a historic haul of treasure, but their team will instantly become the most famous people alive. Probably the most famous ever. If one of them decides they don't like coal, there'll be no coal. If they like coal, that's all we'll use. And that's just coal.

I'm enjoying an eight-minute snooze in the California king-size bed in the penthouse suite of the famed Thompson Hotel located in the heart of Toronto, North America. I might never have been so comfortable. The sheets are of the finest silk. The comforter stuffed to bursting with down. I crack a can of iced coffee. I made sure to bring a whole case. Brewed and canned in the good ol' CUS. I've heard Canada is fine, and the people are fine, but I've heard nothing about their coffee one way or another and don't want to take my chances. Not Today.

"Is it time to get up?" says Kyle, rubbing his eyes and rolling off his trusty cot onto the floor.

"Sure is, sleepy-head. How you doing?"

"Tired. I wish we'd gotten a room with two beds. Or separate rooms even."

"I know, but security. Two rooms means twice the guards. Twice the headaches."

"What about two beds, though?"

"Hey, you want a coffee?"

"Sure. Yeah. That would be fantastic."

"Great. I think there's a Keurig. Boil the water first, though. I don't trust these Canadian sewage systems. Not all scrubbers are created equal, that's what I always say. I think they have hazelnut. But don't quote me. God knows what that means here."

"Thanks," he says, rising with difficulty from the floor.

We are congregated in a boardroom, the Thompson's finest, for the pre-Game briefing. Kyle and I are seated roughly mid-table, polished reclaimed wood in typically pompous Canadian fashion, but I'm fine with it. Again, we're here mostly for promotional purposes.

General Kirkpatrick, seated at one of the heads, begins the meeting. "Well, everyone, we did it." Everyone claps except Kyle, and I side-eye him reproachfully. "But our work isn't done. We gotta think PR. Even if we win, not everyone's going to be happy. Some people – crazy people – think what we're doing is wrong."

"Why? Do these 'crazy people' want a fighting chance?" blurts Kyle, and I check my phone in abject humiliation.

"It's possible, Dr. Ricci. But at the end of the day, today actually, they'll realize it's much easier and far more humane, if there's potential for violent conflict, to file an application with the UN, hammer out the details, and then, like Dr. Martinez says, *game it out.*"

I am given a polite round of applause.

"How is the team looking?" asks a Green Suit, his uniform's left breast a resume of colorful rectangles.

"They're nervous, as expected," says the General. "But our sports psychologists, physical therapists and nutritionists are working with them as we speak. I've no doubt, once The Game starts, they'll be in peak condition mentally and physically. Plus, they're pumped so full of amphetamines they'll be bouncing off the walls for a week."

Everyone laughs.

"Aren't drugs illegal?" asks the big shot with all the rectangles.

"Not if our doctors prescribe them."

"Smart," says Rectangles. "Still, though, I do keep in touch with a few vets from my horse racing days..."

"Copy that," says the General with a wink.

"What's next?"

"Two hours for hair and makeup, then we travel via helicopter to the stadium. The presidents of both countries will be joining us along with our best-trained security personnel and, well, this was going to be a surprise, but also... Bon Jovi!"

The room fucking erupts.

"Settle down, settle down," laughs the General.

"But is that smart?" interrupts Guess Who. "I mean in terms of security. If any of these, uh, 'crazies' want to try something, we could be a target. We are kind of responsible for what's happening."

"Sure," says the General with forced patience. "But that's how it's always been. We'll figure it out. Getting people to hate someone other than us isn't that hard."

"Great point!" I say, rising to my feet and making hard eye contact with Kyle.

Riding the elevator to the roof, I finally start to truly feel the pressure. I've spent so long chasing this damn dream I barely considered achieving it. Sure, either 135 million or close to a billion people are going to die today, over and above the number that would have anyway from things like smallpox and car accidents. So, yeah, it's going to be the bloodiest day in human history. *But* it's going to be followed by, I've calculated, over and over, the least bloody. Same with the day after that and the day after that. The math works, eventually.

I wish Kyle would stop twirling his neck collar. It's making me nervous.

The doors open directly onto the roof, and we are blasted by a wave of cold air. I don't know why anyone would hold a war, digital or otherwise, in a cold-weather country, but that's all above my pay grade, so I don't complain. Kyle is doing enough of that for both of us. Plus, it's amazing what they're doing with parkas these days.

The "whirlybird" is already warming up. Before boarding, I take a moment's respite scanning our host city's skyline. Not bad for a foreign country. A cluster of glimmering skyscrapers reflect the setting sun's pinks and oranges, all punctuated, almost literally, by an exclamation-point-like tower to the south. The last stop before Lake Ontario's whitecap-blasted shores. The gunmetal grey water makes me shiver, just looking at it, so I climb inside, strap into my jump seat. It's incredible how loud these military "choppers" are compared to their commercial counterparts. Yet another reason not to have actual wars. I flash Kyle an "a-okay" sign which he does not return, and I check Wikipedia to see if the gesture has become associated with anything prejudicial. Fuck. It has. Fortunately, no one seems to have noticed, so I resume looking forward to life.

With a jolt, the "eggbeater" rises, slowly at first then faster and faster as if the hand of God is drawing it up, up, up into the sky.

The Hand of God lets go. And we plummet. And I scream and scream until my throat is shredded. The silence is more deafening than the noise because it means the engine has cut out, which means we are going to die. "*Say hello to friends!*" Kyle shouts though I'm not sure if he's preparing to meet loved ones in the Peruvian afterlife or comedically referencing the Hello Friends Mortgage jingle. I think the odds are about even since that's the probability he's going to die today anyway. Drinks, food, tablets and magazines fly everywhere. Passengers make sounds like whale songs. My unstrapped organs rise inside my strapped body. My face slams against my window. The ground approaches faster than I'm used to. Panic overtakes me, and I soil myself, but only slightly, and I plan, if we survive, to immediately exit the "autogiro", fall to the ground, claim a dog has shat there, and demand someone be fired. Bon Jovi just whimpers. The Chinese president tosses him a stress ball.

It bounces off his emaciated chest. We are jolted, hard, and I'm sure the blades are gone and death is imminent. But we are decelerating. Somehow. We have no engine, but we are slowing down.

The ground comes fast, and we land hard but alive. The surviving pilot opens the main hatch, we spill out, and I abort my dog shit plan. For now. I'm too happy to be breathing. So is everyone, except Bon Jovi, who is a hard man to get a handle on. Firefighters race to the scene, spray the flaming engine, and the rotors fall off with dual heavy *clangs*. I approach the shaken pilot, put a hand on his shoulder, ask how the hell he managed that little miracle, and after a moment of perplexed hesitation, he explains "helicopters" can operate without power by feathering the blades a certain way. Before I can ask what the hell feathers have to do with non-avian flighted objects, we are ushered away, and I snatch up an empty french fry container, fill it with my business, and leave it neatly atop a garbage bin none any the wiser.

Gazing up at the stadium, I only now appreciate its enormity, something no model or schematic could convey. An onyx monolith with curving tubes of glowing white, added, at the last minute, to emphasize its almost provocative lines and, ironically, to avoid aircraft disasters. It has been described as everything from "Picasso sculpting obsidian" to "the architectural equivalent of toxic masculinity", but to me, it's just beautiful. The internet has had a field day speculating about who might attend, with many locals predicting none other than the cast of *Degrassi* might show up, including the popular rap musician.

"Makes you feel good, doesn't it? To see it all come together?" I say, but Kyle doesn't hear me. Instead, he asks:

"Can I borrow a pen?"

"What?"

"Can I borrow a pen?" he says louder.

"That's what I thought you said. Sure." I hand him a black Bic. "Don't worry about paying me back. I get them in bulk."

We enter the arena through a strategically non-descript entrance, and like the football stadium, its bowels are mostly concrete. Except here, the walls are lined with images of famous gamers like Ninja and Shroud and HaWskUns. Finally, we reach the main control room, our base of operations. The doors slide open with a satisfying *hiss,* and we enter.

It's game time.

Shit! I should have trademarked that last thought.

The control room is much as I imagined because it was designed that way. Not to look specifically as *I* imagined, but as most people do. Like in an astronaut movie. A big screen up front. Banks of computers operated by scientists wearing headsets. It should make for a great reaction shot if we win. I take note of where the cameras are, trusting my film extra skills to get me in the shot if we do. And if we don't, no harm, no foul, as they used to say. Around the room's periphery are doors leading to washrooms, supply closets and the central mainframe that controls gameplay, collar-management, winner payouts, and calculating concurrent viewers, which are expected to be in the mid-billions. And yeah, that'll be a record.

Right away, Kyle disappears into a washroom. Poor guy must be nervous as all hell. His neck is on the line in more ways than one. But it's just as well. Even though there's a special blast area in the room's southwest corner and accommodations have been made for explosive distancing, I'm fine catching The Game solo.

I hear the gurgle of brewing coffee, but before I can snag a cup, the room starts to shake. What the hell? Is Canada on a fault line? Then the screen flashes to life, displaying a man. But not just any man. It's the same bow-tied lothario employed for championship boxing matches. The crowd roars and stomps their feet. He ambles onto the stage, shining gold mic in hand, draws in a deep breath, and in his rich, silky baritone bellows, "Tonight we will witness the greatest event in the history of sports. The history of entertainment. The history of history. Coming to you live from the neutral site host city of Toronto, North America... Welcome to The Game!" The crowd jumps up and down in, as drone shots reveal, literal waves of churning humanity. He barks his popular copyrighted catchphrase then continues. "This match is scheduled for one fall. The last team with an avatar or avatars remaining will be declared the winner of The Game. Which means they are...?" He holds the sparkling gold mic to the crowd and they shout in unison:

THE...
WINNER...
OF...
THE...
WAR!

He soaks in the accompanying cheers, arms held out wide, then a song I don't recognize blares over the millions of watts of speakers, and he thunders, "First up, weighing a combined 487 pounds... China!" Dozens of dancers wielding Chinese flags enter the arena, moving in perfect sync, followed by the Chinese team themselves. Riding in the backs of Hongqi luxury convertibles, waving to the crowd. The mind boggles at the sponsorship costs for such insane visibility. "First, the sniper. Holder of six world records, nine championship titles and 15 major sponsorships. From Beijing... KlowtiZaurus!" The crowd explodes. KlowtiZaurus wasn't the first gamer to start his YouTube videos with, "Hey, what's up guys," but he certainly popularized it.

"And their strategist, holder of eight world records, 41 championship titles, 23 major sponsorships, inventor of the headshot-rock-ricochet, from Shanghai... JaymeeDeeno!" The crowd, yes, explodes. JaymeeDeeno is the team's "bad boy" *and* "the funny one", which isn't too shabby as far as reputations go. I wish I'd known about the headshot-rock-ricochet thing, though. I wouldn't have added so many rocks to the map if I did.

The announcer pauses, letting the anticipation build, and boy does it. The crowd knows what's coming. "And their commander. Holder of 15 world records, 102 championship titles and over 200 major sponsorships, also from Bejing, the Blaster of Disaster, King of Ping, Headshot Bigshot, Merchant of Merch, Lootin' Rasputin the one and only: Bunnybunnyjumpjump!" The crowd loses whatever remains of their minds. Bunnybunnyjumpjump is far and away the greatest gamer who ever picked up a controller or smashed a key. By any measure, not just sponsorships. His aim, defense and almost supernatural knack for landing in the best, loot-rich locations playing first-person shooters are all second to none. Just the name Bunnybunnyjumpjump strikes fear into the hearts of not just gamers but developers like myself and Kyle – wherever he is, maybe he shouldn't have had all that Canadian coffee – whose job it is to keep things remotely competitive.

Before I can dwell further on Kyle's whereabouts, I hear the opening bars of our team's music, *The Final Countdown,* and the arena erupts into bedlam. It's a great tune, and ordinarily bulletproof entrance music, though I'm not sure going with a band called "Europe" was necessarily right for the occasion. Regardless, it seems like a good time for a bathroom break to complete what the french fry container could not.

I reenter the control room as the screen splits – shout out to our team in the truck, each half displaying a lovingly-crafted three-person hang glider, which the teams pilot into the main playing area. The Game has begun! The graphics are, in all humility, incredible. Not as gritty and realistic as your *Animal Towns,* but likewise, not as cartoonish as, say, *Blood Flood.* We wanted balance. To recognize the horrors of war while maintaining a look and feel our sponsors could get behind.

The Chinese team, or rather their avatars, release from their hang glider, plummet briefly, then pull their parachutes revealing their sponsor logos, which were rumored to cost upward of three billion (yep, with a "b") dollars each, but they're all Chinese companies I've never heard of.

They drop toward Shady Acres, so named after the once-popular rapper Eminem. I have never not disagreed with the branding. Yes, nostalgia sells, but I wanted something modern. Like Taylortown in honor of our finest congressperson. In terms of strategy, however, it's a solid choice. There's plenty of buildings, which we've branded "recording studios", though programming-wise, they're basically houses combined with racquetball courts. You're liable to get sniped there later, with all the high ground, but during early stages, there ought to be plenty of loot. And seriously, who am I to argue with the immortal Bunnybunnyjumpjump?

Then the building shakes, though I know by now it's no earthquake. The Camericans have dropped at the *exact same spot*. This was not expected. Jesus. We designed the map specifically to play into a variety of player strengths. In the case of our guys, I thought for sure they'd choose Mount Rushmore. Not the popular tourist spot, of course. There's no reason to promote a foreign country. I believe it was named after that Bill Murray movie where he plays a sexual deviant. Regardless, I feel a profound sense of loss. Unless something goes horribly right, most of the map we've painstakingly constructed won't come into play at all.

The Chinese team lands and the screen splits into four windows, one displaying the still descending Camerican team (their parachutes sponsored by McDonald's, Tesla, and the latest *Fast and Furious* movie) with the others fixed on the Chinese combatants as they spread out using the Giersdorf technique as many, including myself, predicted. Despite the stakes, I cannot help but marvel at the graphics! Even the lighting is top-notch, with every leaf on every tree impacting how the rays travel through its branches. Same with the dust on the windows. Hell, even the dust in the air.

The Camerican team lands shockingly close to their opponents, again, according to expectations. The environment looks pretty much identical to where Team China landed, and I pray that viewers don't think the whole map looks like that. It doesn't even snow in Shady Acres! God knows how many hours we wasted toiling away on snow, making sure it fell at just the right speed, added the exact proper slipperiness to the ground. We even made a deal with a prominent personal injury law firm. Any headshot executed while the player's avatar was slipping and/or falling would be designated the "Gonzales,

Smith, Varadkar and Associates Slip and Fall Headshot of the Game", but so much for that.

The Camericans land and the screen splits into six. I chuckle, thinking how confusing this must be for viewers not accustomed to gaming spectatorship, though I am comforted knowing they'll catch up after a few wars. Maybe revealing only a small part of the map will work out after all – we'll need less new content in the future, which means less work, but crucially, according to our three war contract, just as much moolah.

The first few minutes, for once, go as anticipated, with players occupied locating loot boxes containing all manner of weapons, armor, ammo and medical supplies. At first, players can expect to find weapons produced in their respective countries, but there is nothing stopping, say, a Camerican player looting a fallen enemy and taking their QBB-95 Bullpup light machine gun (a variant of the QBZ-95) with a 5.8x42mm DBP87 magazine. China makes fine weapons, but they have a long way to go as far as branding is concerned, with all due-

A blinding flash emanates from two of the six screens. When it subsides, both ToTLee and JaymeeDeeno are gone. Replaced by smoldering craters. What the hell? There's no nukes in The Game. Not even rocket launchers. I made sure of it. We wanted to ensure fair and viewer-friendly combat, not a quick slaughter. Something that would last between 90 minutes and two hours, AKA the sweet spot. There is another flash, and KlowtiZaurus is gone. So is ButrFethRz. Just more smoldering craters. Only two avatars remain, LaZrFAce and Bunnybunnyjumpjump.

A tremendous *roar*, more a *growl*, erupts from the speakers, and a shadow falls over everything. The ground shakes slightly underfoot, and a lot on screen, as an enormous, digital, metallic foot drops from the sky, landing with a thunderous *boom*, almost crushing both players and taking out a strategically dilapidated liquor store intended to evoke Eminem's Detroit. The crowd cheers and cheers.

"Kyle! Kyle!" I shout, but he is nowhere to be found.

Another "foot" crashes down atop a rusty old Ford Aerostar. It explodes.

"Kyle! What's going on! What is all this?"

He doesn't answer, but The Game's "camera" does. It tilts up, revealing a mechanical dinosaur. It must have 10,000 individual moving parts. The detail is phenomenal. But that's not what catches my eye. It's the ro-beast's head. It's Kyle! His face anyway. Ro-Kyle *roars* and a laser shoots from his mouth, cutting through Shady Acres like a blazing hot knife. Bunnybunnyjumjump leaps to safety just in time, but LaZrFAce is incinerated along with her meticulously designed and researched loot. At least, I thought Bunnybunnyjumpjump escaped the blast, but his avatar collapses, rolls over, and I see the entire back of him is gone. Incinerated. Leaving just charred, smoking meat that I do not recall programming.

Then the screen goes blank, and all I can do is gape like a rube. My stomach clenches into knots. Finally, the screen lights up displaying the results:

Camerica: Three kills.

China: Three kills.

It's a tie. But how? That's impossible. Even if two players shoot and kill each other simultaneously, we can still calculate which bullet struck first. But lasers, as any good scientist knows, travel faster than bullets and it's much, much harder to measure their fucking velocity.

The mystery of Kyle's whereabouts is resolved when he emerges from what I now realize was not a bathroom but the system's central mainframe. They need to label these doors better. "Kyle, what's going on?" I shout as scientists race for the exits. "What's with that giant robot dinosaur thing? And why is your face on it? And what happened to your neck collar?"

Boom! The not-a-bathroom door is blown off its hinges. His collar exploding? I can't be sure, but I have my suspicions.

"Change of plans," he says.

"I can see that. It's a tie. Do you realize what that means?"

"Yes. Obviously. That's why the plans were changed."

"But now everyone's going to die on both sides. A billion people. Why?"

"I can answer that," says General Kirkpatrick, entering from either a bathroom or the central mainframe. "You didn't really think you could actually end all war, did you?"

"That's exactly what I thought. I didn't know that wasn't understood."

"It was not. This is all more an advertisement for how badly needed actual war really is and what can go wrong when you try to fix what isn't broken."

"I think it's kind of broken."

"Let me ask you, what is the point of war? Why does it happen?"

"Religion. Every war is caused by religion. Everyone knows that."

"Name one."

I think for a moment. "The Crusades?"

"I mean recently."

"The Crusades are recent on a long enough timeline."

"Think harder."

I do, and it comes to me in a flash. "War is good business..."

"Exactly."

"Even still, how did you change the programming? Even Kyle doesn't have the-"

"That I can answer," says another voice, and I turn to see the man about my size with whom I almost collided earlier at the Pentagon, still wearing the blazer I thought looked like mine, but I now realize is mine – the one I'd worn to Congress before being strip-searched and hosed down. He holds up my speech, which in retrospect, was unnecessarily detailed and also written on the back of a print-out of all my passwords.

"You stole my speech! And passwords! And blazer!"

"Looks good, doesn't it?"

"Yeah, really makes your eyes pop. But that's not the point!"

Above the control room, I can hear explosions going off one by one and try not to picture the human heads flying around like confetti. On a day when a lot of people were scheduled to die for the betterment of humankind, a shitload are dying for no reason whatsoever. My knees buckle, and I slump to the floor. Kyle smirks, approaches, looking down at me in every way possible.

"Why, Kyle?" I plead.

"Money, obviously."

"You have money. Or at least would have. I told you this was going to bring you a ton of exposure."

"Oh yeah, *exposure*. You get the results, I get vague promises of... I don't even know what."

"You're not a materialistic person. Money can't be the only reason."

"It isn't. Also, I hate you."

"Why? I'm a nice guy." I cringe, realizing that's the last thing a genuinely nice guy would ever say.

"Well, for one, you're a raging narcissist."

"I am not!" I spit without contemplating his words. I have an enormous ego that protects me from the parts of reality I don't like, but I'm no narcissist.

"Yes, you are. You're a condescending, manipulative prick. I knew it the first day we met on that bench."

"You know what? You're right. I'm sorry," I say, looking him hard in the eye. "I'm sorry you wrongly think that. But if you do, even if it's not true, I'll change. Or at least, try to change the perception-"

"Shut up! Please. For once in your bafflingly charmed idiot life!"

I do.

"And that's not even all."

"Oh, come on! That's already a lot."

"You're also kind of racist."

"Bite your forked Peruvian tongue! Where do you get that?"

"Well, I'm not Peruvian!"

"Then what are you?" I counter, though again, not the words of a traditionally great person.

"Italian! Did you not notice I have spaghetti for lunch pretty much every day?"

"I thought they were noodles."

"They are noodles!"

"I'm so confused."

"I know you are, *boss*. That's how we were so sure this would work."

General Kirkpatrick jumps in. "Let's go, Kyle. We need to get to the bunkers."

"Bunkers?" I say, looking up from the floor AKA "Da Kyle Zone".

"That's right. You didn't think this would end with just a billion dead? As we speak, generals on both sides are blaming each other and preparing full-scale nuclear assaults on strategic locations around the world, including..." She points upward, then continues. "Come on, Kyle. Last one in the pool's a rotten egg."

"Wait!" I wail. "There has to be something we can do. Can't we contact China and explain what happened? They'll understand. They're very..." I trail off, not wanting to touch another racial nerve.

"They might. That is, if they weren't in on it. Which they are."

"Then take me with you! I'm a good swimmer. I can be a lifeguard! I can swim a whole lap underwater."

"A whole lap?"

"A whole lap!"

"Of an Olympic-sized pool?"

"Well, not *Olympic-sized*..."

"Let's get out here."

A sense of *deja vu* overcomes me, and I am taken back to my childhood when similar words were frequently uttered by classmates who'd never be friends. The General exits, followed by the guy about my size. Kyle, however, hangs back. "It was great working with you, Edgar. Thanks for the opportunity."

"Go to hell."

"Maybe someday. Enjoy your last bit of life, though. I've taken the liberty of setting up a game you can play while the missiles get here."

"Yeah? What game?"

"*Missile Command.*"

"You cheeky bastard!"

Kyle grins and turns to leave.

"Wait!" I shout. "There's one thing I gotta know."

"Better make it quick. My pneumatic tube awaits," he says, barely breaking stride. I don't even recognize him anymore, and not just because he's not Peruvian.

"How did you get the collar off?"

He chuckles. "Easy. The company that makes them also does bike locks, which you can easily pick with one of these." He tosses me my black Bic, which I do not catch, and it bounces away, disappearing under a workstation. I follow its path into darkness, and when I look up, Kyle is gone.

I rise and race around the room, hauling on doors, but they're locked. All of them. Even the bathrooms. "Busy!" someone shouts as I bang on the last of them, but I leave them be. Might as well let the poor sap die in peace doing probably what they do best.

Everything is now silent. Even the stadium above. Everyone with a head has probably been trampled, or in a few cases, escaped. Not that it will matter much when a multi-megaton nuclear warhead with a multi-kilometer blast radius shows up to say hello.

With nothing else to do, I head to the front of the room, where a classic NES system complete with a vacuum tube television is waiting along with a slip of paper. I pick it up and read:

"Fava beans, white bread, skim milk..."

I don't read the rest. Just pick up a controller. It feels good in my hands. Reminds me of when I was a kid and would game all day without a care in the world.

Almost instantly, I lose.

These old games are hard.

I select "Play Again" and-

(*static*)

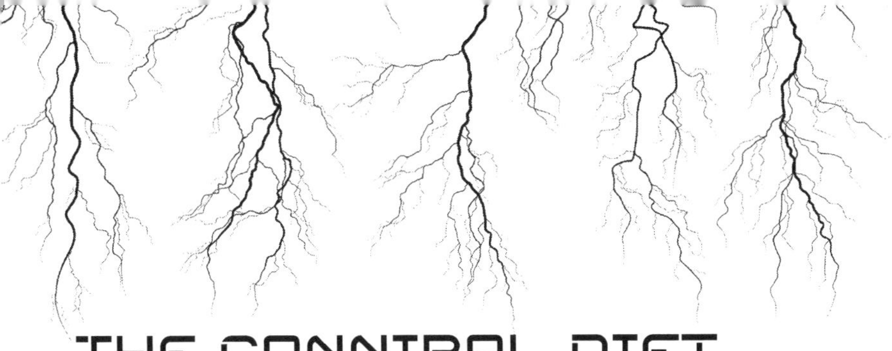

THE CANNIBAL DIET

By
Dr. Cassandra Picton

Editor's Note: The following essay/prophecy of doom is derived from two sources, both, thankfully, physical pages, which I have edited together in the interests of clarity. The first is a diary written by hand in what tests have confirmed is human blood. Call it "Blood Diary". The second consists of excerpts from a book, The Cannibal Diet, which has sold, or rather will sell, according to the large, aggressive cover text, "Billions and Billions of Copies!"

Blood Diary: Part One

Nov 23, 2043

Over a decade has elapsed since my book, *The Cannibal Diet*, became a global sensation. It received praise from critics and scientists alike, hailed as a "dietary revolution", "a new way forward" and "the book we need right now", though it was never meant to be any of those things. Jonathan Swift once wrote of satire, it is "a kind of mirror where everyone sees anything but not himself", and I now realize he was right. Who would have thought the guy who wrote *Gulliver's Travels* would know anything about satire? But back then, my confidence in my fellow humans was ludicrously high. I thought it would be obvious I was not actually advocating cannibalism. You'd think the cover art, a cartoon woman in a praying mantis costume eating and tastefully making love to her mate with a voice bubble reading "Yum! Yum!" would have made that clear. But human logic, it turns out, is not Logical. At least, not in any grand Platonic sense. My heavily pockmarked and scarred tongue will not stop bleeding.

<u>*The Cannibal Diet*: Introduction</u>

Growing up, like so many others, I never met the usual standards of physical beauty. I was overweight, out of shape and had skin like a bowl of raspberries in heavy cream. Suffice to say, I was bullied and mercilessly so. The other children, with their impossibly skinny bodies, would point at me and shout "fatty, fatty, fat, fat" and other mantras thought hilarious by those chanting them. But it wasn't hilarious to me. Just more fuel for my insecurities, which caused me to eat more, which made me more insecure. Many of you will know what I'm talking about.

Starting in my teenage years, I tried every diet under the sun. The Elimination Diet. Weight Watchers. Cleanses. But nothing worked. They were all, in my eyes, just eating disorders with a haircut. No matter how hard I tried, the fat refused to melt away. Exercise helped but not much. I'd wake up before the sun, pull on my off-brand trainers, bundle up in clothing marketed as adventurous, and set out for a jog that accomplished nothing but adding physical anguish to my mental woe.

University was better but not much. I studied nutrition and kinesiology (with a minor in poli-sci) at the University of North Carolina, and though my classmates tried to be kind, I could tell how they looked at me with eyes perched upon towering, muscular bodies that I was the "Other". Someone to be accepted because it was the politically correct thing to do. Yet, their overly enthusiastic approval constituted a form of rejection in its own right. The day I was voted "Most Slim and Attractive" was among the worst of my life, however well-meaning the gesture may have been.

Even worse was the growing sense that nothing I learned was relevant to my plight. There was an almost cult-like devotion to old chestnuts like The Food Pyramid, which only exemplified and perpetuated the corporate domination of our food supply. Wheat producers hawking genetically modified wares that spike blood sugar levels and promote newfangled allergies. Dairy farmers lobbying for increased puss limits in the milk, cheese, Kumis and yogurt we feed our children. Fruit and vegetable megacorporations dependent on indentured servitude. Then there's animal meat. Pushed on us by Big Meat, some of the most powerful corporations in the world with tentacles reaching right up to the President. Right up to the Queen. And beyond.

Now, it should be clear from our title, *The Cannibal Diet*, that it is not meat itself that is the problem. It's the source.

Consider the following, which I hope you will since it's the only useful information I gleaned paying $40,000 a year in tuition. Meat protein, it turns out, consists of 20 amino acids, nine of which are essential for human beings. Like valine, leucine and isoleucine. The problem is balance. Each animal's flesh contains amino acids in different proportions, none of which are precisely equivalent to that found in human anatomy. I repeat and italicize: *none.*

According to the most recent and authoritative studies, a non-cannibalistic human, in order to take in all necessary amino acids, must consume the following meat products *per day*:

- Beef: 18 oz
- Pork: 16 oz
- Chicken: 22 oz
- Fish (farmed): 11 oz
- Fish (wild): 6 oz
- Bison and Buffalo: 10 oz
- Turkey: 5 oz
- Pythons and Other Constrictors: 5 oz
- Elk: 8 oz

That's a lot of meat and probably more than most readers eat in a week, let alone a day. Again, it's important to note that the issue isn't getting enough protein, it's getting the right proteins in the proper combinations. The bottom line? Your hunger cannot be sated be through a normal diet, but it sure as barbecue sauce can be via a cannibalistic one.

<u>Blood Diary: Part Two</u>

In truth, I was never overweight. I *earned* that "Most Slim and Attractive" award. At my peak, I was an elite athlete who hadn't consumed an ounce of meat since my 10th birthday. I'll never forget that day. I'd determined and informed my family that I was officially to become a vegetarian and wanted a vegan birthday cake. Yet, as my friends sang *Happy Birthday*, and I could see the glow of candles foreshadowing my mother's arrival from the kitchen, I could tell something was wrong. Or, more accurately, I could smell it. Moments later, my mother entered carrying a pewter tray on which was the largest and bloodiest piece of meat (bison, I think) I'd ever seen. The others erupted in celebration and tore into the (probably) bison like dingoes happening upon a fresh kill. Still, I felt no ill will toward my mother, even after she held me down so my friends could take turns shoving meat in my face. After all, she was subject to the same lies and propaganda as everyone else.

The Cannibal Diet: Nature's Choice (Chapter 1)

The fact it is impossible to obtain a healthy balance of protein through a normal diet does not mean all is lost. On the contrary! And this is where cannibalism comes in. I know, I know. "Cannibalism is wrong!" you might be thinking, clutching your pearls and that picture of grandma, imagining a hungry mob knocking down her door, torches in hand, desperate for that perfect balance of amino acids. Ready to fry her up like so much pig bacon. But fear not. No one is coming for grandma. And if they do, well, "from each according to his ability..."

Consider the history.

Cannibalism goes back to ancient times. Before history was even history. That is to say, no one wrote anything down because there was no writing. How then do we know cannibalism was widely practiced? Bones! Bones are the textbooks of the past, able to tell us all kinds of things about the people who used them to hold children and kick stones. In fact, there is an entire field of study on the topic called "osteology", which helps scientists called "archaeologists" determine things like whether a bone came from a male or female. Adolescent or adult. Even if their former owners suffered from headaches, which we see evidence of in the form of "trephination", that is, cutting out palm-sized chunks of skull to relieve pressure and allow whatever demons not shrewd enough to find the ears, nose, anus or eyes to escape.

Most importantly, bones paint a picture of how the person died, whether through "natural" causes like cancer or buffalo goring or ending up in the stomachs of family and friends. A clue that points to the latter, that the person died playing the most important role possible in a cannibalistic community, is the presence of cuts, which occur when flesh is carved from the bones. Another is teeth marks. Interestingly, we find evidence of both human and canine teeth marks in the archaeological record, which is how we know dogs have been a domesticated friend to humans for thousands of years!

Even now, you might be thinking, "But Cassandra! I learned from Hobbes (the human) that the State of Nature is 'nasty, brutish and short'. Does that not suggest cannibalism was practiced out of necessity, when no other food options were available, rather than as a normal part of a healthy diet?" The simple answer is "nope!"

All the proof you need can be found in the Bible. Of course, not all readers are religious, and I make no warranties here pertaining to the existence or nonexistence of God. For more on that, be sure to check out my colleague Betty Fankraker's wonderful book *A Horse Walks into a Bar... And it's God!* For us, what's important about the Bible is how darn long people lived back then. In one case, Methuselah – son of Enoch who begot Lamech who begot Noah (!) – we find a man who lived to the ripe old age of 969, which is 847 years longer than the oldest modern human. Of course, there are many reasons for these long lifespans, like the lack of pollution and cell phone tower radiation, but the primary explanation is cannibalism.

Still not convinced? *Still* thinking, you stubborn goose, "But Cassandra! These were God-fearing people, and does God not tell us in Genesis that 'whoever sheds human blood, by humans shall their blood be shed; for in the image of God has God made Mankind'?" He sure does! But keep in mind, while the words "blood" and "shed", when combined, have come to be viewed, in modern usage, as "any act that results in the shedding of blood", we need to remember, in Biblical times, the word "bloodshed" was understood more like how "murder" is today. You couldn't just kill someone willy-nilly, but if there's protein factors involved? People are definitely *on the table* as far as God is concerned.

Blood Diary: Part Three

Within a month, *The Cannibal Diet* had sold, in various formats, 5.5 billion copies worldwide, making it the top-selling book in history, ironically supplanting the Bible atop this prestigious list. It was the Number One best-seller in every country but Britain, where the latest *Harry Potter* clung precipitously to the pole position, though I and others suspected most copies were purchased by JK Rowling herself and buried somewhere discreet within driving distance of London.

The first royalty cheque was enough to cover my credit card debts and the down payments on several houses, and practically overnight, I went from a struggling nutritionist and cross-fit instructor to probably the most famous author, nay person, who ever lived. Eat your heart out Sir Albert Yankovic! I was the toast of the town, appearing on *Late Night with Jimmy Kimmel*, *The Macauly Culkin Show*, and could often be found at Oprah Winfrey's famous all-night sex orgies, fuelled as they were by the trendiest narcotics. I texted regularly with the Sultan of Brunei, just about life.

Looking back, I might have suspected something was wrong after a debaucherous night of hot tubbing with the (original!) cast of *Friends*. We'd been drinking hard liquor and doing circles of the best chunk to ever come out of Madagascar when their butler, one of the Hanks offspring, I believe, approached carrying a platter of snacks, not an unusual sight at a party, but there was something about the way the Friends attacked the food that gave me pause. Celebrities rarely eat, and never so voraciously. No utensils or napkins. Just a frenzy of feeding. Loud grunts and belches. It was behavior I'd come to expect from Courtney Cox but not the rest. And where was Matt LeBlanc? He was never one to miss a snack. Pondering this, I snatched up a piece of floating meat, which had somehow survived the gastrointestinal onslaught, and popped it in my mouth. Of course, I was too high on chunk to know it, but I had just ingested human flesh.

They called it "The Joey Special".

The next morning, I awoke feeling wonderful. Chunk, as they say, is a helluva drug. Still, I decided to sleep a little more, so kicked David Schwimmer out of my bed, tipping him a heavy gold bar for his generous contribution to my sexual gratification, and he left galloping on all fours and neighing like a horse per my instructions. I was on top of the world, literally, having had my home suspended by hot air balloons (the San Fernando Valley is gorgeous from such a vantage), and smiled, peering out the window, watching David's parachute open, silently offering him props for having commissioned a chute design based on the "Caesar" haircut he once popularized.

"I wonder if he calculated the weight of the gold?" I thought, turned from the window and checked my phone to find dozens of emails. Apparently, people were taking my book seriously. Or were they? No, I thought, that can't be possible. They must be playing along. People are smart. In hindsight, it's ironic I managed to convince myself no one was eating humans when I was, at that moment, digesting a piece of Matt LeBlanc, but that's the thing about the rich and famous. We have egos, and sometimes they get in the way of our judgment.

The Cannibal Diet: It's the Ingredients, Stupid (Chapter 2)

By this point, having educated yourself about cannibalism's misunderstood history, you should be ready to choose health over prejudice. There is no greater sign of intelligence than the willingness to admit one is wrong, and I applaud you for making the effort. It's really no different than how surgeons once refused to wash their hands because, as one Englishman famously quipped, "A gentleman's hands are always clean." They didn't know about things like bacteria back then, just like you probably didn't know about amino acids.

This does not, however, mean that all men (or women!) are created equal. Just as not every cow gets to be Kobe beef or every duck *foie gras*. Criteria you should therefore consider when deciding who to eat (or not!) are:

Are they related to me?

Pop quiz, Hot Shot: do the same factors that make procreation undesirable among people with similar genes apply to their consumption? The simple answer is "Nope!" Oftentimes, it is the people closest to us whose amino acid proportions are most similar to ours and therefore best to eat.

Are they a smoker, drinker or chunk-head?

If so, stay away! Would you eat a piece of charcoal? Of course not, unless you were "all chunked up" and needed a good stomach pumping.

Are they athletic?

Athletes are typically the most nutritious but be wary of marathon runners, triathletes and steeplechasers who are mostly gristle and promote flatulence.

Are they the same race, religion or ethnicity as me?

I'm not touching that one!

Are they smart?

As with athletes, smarter people typically make the best meal options. Just don't eat the brain (see below).

Do they read or write poetry?

These people should be killed but not eaten.

Are they likable?

The jury is still out on this one, but I would recommend avoiding those impure of spirit, the reason being, DNA can be altered, according to recent studies, by unhealthy behavior, and could similarly impact those who consume it.

Blood Diary: Part Four

It was Chapter 2 of *The Cannibal Diet* and its tendency to be wildly misinterpreted that caused, as they used to say on the Gladwell Compound before The Hunger took over, the point to tip. The family unit is the foundation of modern society, and, it turns out, is substantially weakened by interfamilial consumption. Similarly, the mandate I established to eat only the smartest and strongest left only the dumb and infirm. But it was my recommendation we eat the nice that proved most fatal. If the family is society's foundation, then politeness is its superstructure. Saying "please" and "thank you" and, most of all, "sorry". How many non-nutritionally beneficial killings could have been prevented with a simple, "Sorry about your Uncle Bert, but you know, amino acids, right?"

Without getting into the truly sordid details, the following is a timeline, to the best of my recollection, of my dizzying rise and catastrophic fall.

Dec 31, 2033

11:54 PM

I email my completed manuscript six minutes before its January 1, 2034 deadline.

11:56 PM

I email my completed manuscript revised so my name is spelled correctly.

11:57 PM

I email my completed manuscript revised so that goddamn comma on page 243 is taken out and cast into punctuation hell, the same pit of misery I've been mired in for the last three months during the editing process.

11:58 PM

I start drinking.

11:59 PM

I check my email one last time and see all my messages have bounced back. Upon further inspection, I see, due to an autofill error, I have sent the lot to a defunct work account belonging to my ex, Willy, and not my agent at the William Morris Agency. I feel humiliation and relief, then send my manuscript to the proper account as the clock strikes midnight.

Jan 1, 2034

8:32 AM

I wake up still clutching a half-empty 40 oz bottle of peach schnapps and promise myself I'll never, ever drink again.

8:33 AM
I start drinking.

Jan 2, 2034

I wake up still clutching some stud.

Jan 3, 2034

I check my email. There are 15 messages from my agent, Charles. In the first, she informs me she has received my manuscript and forwarded it to the copyeditors. So far, they have found it free of error except for a missed comma on page 243, and I smash my laptop against my desk until it is a twisted mass of junk. I read the rest on my phone. Mostly contract stuff, plus an email telling me the copyeditors have revised their position on the comma and taken it out.

Jan 15, 2034

I receive word that my book is headed to the printers and should be ready in time for the pre-Valentines Day diet rush, which usually begins around February 10. In my excitement, I do not remind my agent that my book is satirical and not to be taken seriously. Why kill the momentum? Plus, people are smart. They'll get it.

Feb 1, 2034

I start my promotional tour on The Oprah Winfrey show. I'm a touch nervous, having never been on television, let alone something broadcast internationally to a legion of fans, virtually all of whom need some nutritional guidance. Plus, I've heard Oprah is a fierce interviewer. All fastballs. Nothing but heat. I do, however, love how the makeup makes me look 10 years younger, even if it does give me the complexion of a sex doll. The good kind you find at the nicer shag parlors, but still.

Oprah "warms up" the crowd juggling a set of bowling pins on a unicycle while absolutely crushing the "Always Be Closing" monologue from *Glengarry Glen Ross*. The crowd explodes with adulation.

Finally, it's my time. My time to shine.

Oprah stands center-stage, posture perfect and smile warm. She introduces me. I take the stage to wild applause but am blinded by the hot stage lights. Trying vainly to shield my eyes, panic starts to overtake me, but it's not far to the couch, and I manage to reach it and sit down without incident. I wouldn't be the first to see my career crumble on its cushions. She begins the interview.

Oprah: Cassandra, welcome. Thanks for coming on the show.

Me: Thanks for having me.

Oprah: Let's get right down to it. Tell me about your new book. Not that it needs much of an introduction, everyone's talking about it.

Audience Member: You go, girl!

A door flies open, and a team of security guards enter and drag the screaming audience member out by his beard. This will later, per Oprah's policy on crowd violence, be edited out and the footage destroyed.

Me: Well, Oprah, it's a diet book. But not just any diet book. Not like the rest, which in most cases are just eating disorders with a haircut.

Audience: Ha, ha, ha. Ha?

Oprah: Like which diets?

Me: Well, any of the ones where you don't eat for a week.

There is a *whooshing* sound from the audience as several offending diet books are set on fire at once.

Oprah: Right, but what makes yours different?

Me: It's all about protein balance (here I discuss amino acids for 17 solid minutes. None of it is usable. I'm losing the audience, so I improvise. This, as it turns out, was a mistake). Also, uh, it's great for the environment.

The audience bathes me in adoration, and Oprah is pleased.

I wasn't wrong, by the way. Environmentally speaking, there are clearly too many of us. Just there's a good time and bad time to bring certain things up. Like when people are on the edge of the fence about cannibalism and looking for an excuse?

That's a bad time.

Feb 2, 2034

Oprah sends me a personal email informing me my book is to become an official "O-Club" selection, though I fail, at first, to grasp the inherent double entendre.

Feb 9, 2034

Charles emails me some pre-sale figures, which I conclude are erroneous. There's no way a billion people had the foresight and financial capacity to place a pre-order.

Feb 10, 2034

I am awoken by a reversing Brinks truck pulling into my driveway, step outside, and see the first skid of 100s land on the asphalt, cracking it. That's a lot of moolah just sitting there. Thinking fast, and to throw my neighbor off the scent, I shout with exaggerated volume, "Thanks for dropping off the, uh... pieces of stinky dog shit." The Brinks guy gives me a wink. This isn't his first rodeo.

Feb 13, 2034

Just for fun, I Google *The Cannibal Diet.* The result is barely something I recognize as a number. I repeat the search, but this time, put "*The Cannibal Diet*" in quotes. Somehow, there's even more. I click on the first article written by a *New Yorker* columnist who claims to have been on *The Cannibal Diet* for just two days and already lost six pounds while running his first ever sub-four-minute mile at age 71. I laugh. If anyone is likely to appreciate satire, it's the men and women of letters at the *New Yorker*. Relieved, I open a dating app for rich people and scroll through looking for "company" for tomorrow.

Feb 14, 2034

I enter Nobu's Malibu location through the celebrity entrance and am escorted to a table where Congressperson Taylor Lautner is already seated, looking, as always, gorgeous. We hug. His body is like a rock, and his suit smells of freshly tanned leather. I ask him, "What is that fabulous suit you're wearing?"

He answers, "Tom Ford" with a cryptic smile I interpret as flirtatious.

We make small talk about life, sipping peach schnapps martinis until our food arrives. I'm not much for sushi, but the meal is delicious, and afterward, I feel incredible. Strong.

It must be the schnapps.

Later, in the parking lot, we make out heavily, ignoring the flashbulbs of paparazzi. He invites me back to his beach house to "check out his Oscars", but I decline. We both know there's another date in our future, and it's going to be a flat-out shag-fest.

Feb 15, 2034

My phone *dings.* A message from Taylor. I check it. It's a dick pic, which is great, ordinarily, but I sense it's not his. At least, I hope not. Typically, when someone sends you a picture of their old chap, it's attached to their body. This must be a prop from his Oscar-nominated film, *Who Greased the Hatchets?*

Feb 16, 2034

I receive word from my real estate agent that Stephen Spielberg has finally cracked under the weight of my offer and agreed to sell me his house and everything in it. I reply (after a bit) that I am excited to own an original Chewbacca costume. She replies (immediately), saying *Star Wars* was made by George Lucas. I respond (after a bit), "Well, buy his house too!" She responds (immediately) that *Star Wars* is now owned by Disney, so I go ahead and purchase the company using a finance app I apparently drunk-bought at some point. It's going to be a fun Halloween!

Feb 18, 2034

I am jolted from a dream about smoking a nice Montecristo #1 by a loud *crash.* I elevate the bed. Hydraulics *hiss* and I ride the momentum through the door, grabbing the machete I keep leaned against the dresser just in case. I make several wrong turns before arriving in the main foyer/secondary piano room. Glass covers the floor along with a brick I don't remember putting there. I rush to the window and see an enormous, black pickup truck – talk about sending a Freudian message loud and clear – skidding down the street blaring its horn, a Dixie version of La Cucaracha.

I drop the machete, pick up the brick, and see a small note affixed to it, which reads:

Thanx fr da fomble, azzhole!!!!

I realize with relief the brick was not meant for me but my next-door neighbor. And like clockwork, a gorgeous 6'4 stud with a chiseled jaw and confident eyes – I think his name is "Tom" or perhaps "Thom" – appears before me, clutching a slip of paper of his own.

"I think this is yours," he says with a voice like gravel and silk, slipping me his piece and ignoring my offer of reciprocation. It reads:

This iz ur falt...

"This could be for anyone," I say flirtatiously.

"Turn it over," he replies. Just normal. I think.

I do and see a picture of myself, or at least my head, photo-shopped onto an image I find repugnant in a way that's impossible to convey in a non-visual, unscented medium. I look up hopefully; maybe he's flirting after all, reasoning I can get used to just about anything when it comes to the sack, but he is gone.

I head to the nearest wall screen and scroll through my news feed. There are many, many articles about murder. Bodies mangled, found in various pieces in various places. Horrible stuff. I click "sports", hoping to take my mind off things. According to the *Iceland Review,* the organizers of the World's Strongest Man competition have issued a press release stating their servers have crashed and hard. Probably hackers. That, or a million people signed up on the same day with verified 900-pound max bench presses. "Curiouser and curiouser..." I mutter, unconcerned with plagiarizing *Alice in Wonderland* since I now own the company that owns the IP.

Feb 20, 2034

2:24 PM

I order sushi, something I now have a ravenous appetite for, and it takes over four hours to arrive. I consider not tipping the delivery person but decide against it when I notice the driver's side of their 1984 Chevette Scooter tilts down appreciably as it pulls up the driveway, only to rock back to about level when one of the most muscular women I've ever seen exits, brown bags in hand. She thunders up the walk, presses the doorbell. The loud Wookie yell startles us both, but I quickly recover and tell her to please leave the bags on the porch.

2:26 PM

The sushi is delicious. Not fishy at all. I make a mental note to purchase steel chopsticks since I keep snapping the wood ones.

Feb 21, 2034

11:00 AM

My alarm goes off, and I immediately burst into an uncontrollable fit of laughter that lasts 15 minutes. Oh, Christ. This could get me into hot water intellectual property-wise. I rise from bed and instantly fall to the ground, my body wracked by tremors. Once they subside, I pull myself to my feet, relieved. The fit should sufficiently differentiate what just happened to qualify as an original idea. Suffice to say, I'll not be wearing clown makeup any time soon.

I head to the kitchen and make a breakfast sushi smoothie, leaving out the rice and seaweed and fried yams and sesame seeds and avocado and wasabi and pickled ginger and soy sauce. I drink it all in one gulp, wipe my face and gaze at my reflection in a wall tablet. My teeth are stained bright red like I'm some kind of wine drunk. Which I am, but still. It's disgusting, and I decide to do something about it.

11:05 AM

In the master bathroom, I stare hard into the mirror. "Disgusting. Disgusting," I mutter, bringing a rusty wood file to my mouth, place it between two incisors, and I start to saw back and forth. The pain is immense but necessary, like a cold shower after a hard workout, and I take satisfaction in the small pile of tooth dust growing into a little mountain in the sink.

Several agonizing hours later, I rinse my mouth and spit out what looks like a mix of cherry Kool-Aid and sand. My face is on fire. The half bottle of peach schnapps did nothing, nor did the other half. Or maybe it did. It's not like I have a familiar baseline for what pain level I'm supposed to experience sawing my teeth into pointy tips.

Feb 22, 2034

Feeling sexier than I ever have following my auto-dental endeavor, I watch various versions of *The Most Dangerous Game*. Aside from, of course, the one with the guy from *Inglorious Basterds* and the Stephen Baldwin-equivalent Helmsworth. Each is electrifying, and between viewings, I putter around the house looking for bladed weapons.

I check my email. Nothing but spam. Honestly, how stupid do these scammers think I am? Like I'm going to click on a link with some made-up subject like "Hundreds of Millions Dead Or Missing". If you're going to fabricate something, at least make it semi-believable.

Oh hell. I'll click just one. I have lots of computers and can handle one getting some weird virus. It's from the *New*

York Times, so should at least be good for a laugh. The article reads: "Te werlud marns azz ullmist ereriwon huz biin eetun or incipizitatud by bodi trenurs, pathilujikal ootbirsts of lafffur n uthur simtims of Coorroo dzeez. Manni r blaamn won purrsin spusifikily..."

Jesus. This is crap, even for the *Times.* Where are they getting these writers? I continue reading: "Kyzandyrha Pitin, awetur uv tu itt buuk 'Tuhu Kanibil Dyit'..."

Unreadable tripe, I think, head to the master bedroom, lie down on the Cali king-size bed and smoke a big fat cigar.

The Cannibal Diet: The Choicest Cuts and Fun Recipes to Try at Home! (Chapter 3)

Before we get to the many mouthwatering ways human meat can be prepared, let's briefly go through the different cuts and how they are best enjoyed.

- Neck: Try it diced in a nice Hungarian goulash.
- Shoulder: Great for steaks, though should be slow-cooked. The shoulder is a working muscle and takes some effort to tenderize.
- Middle of Loin: Now we're talking! Use the highly versatile mid-loin for all your favorite dishes.
- Lower Loin: Think T-bone steak, but that's actually good for you.
- Arms (Lower): This meat is tough and best reserved for soups.
- Arms (Upper): Prepare in the same way you would a lamb shank.
- Legs (Lower): Sinew city! Toss 'em in the pot with the lower arms.
- Legs (Thigh): Another working muscle. Slow cooker to the rescue!

- Buttocks (Topside or Silverside): Makes a great slow roast.
- Lungs: Packed with iron! Great for those with iron deficiencies like hemophiliacs and vegetarians.
- Skin: High in fat but adds crispiness to any meal, especially when fried. Make sure to wash and shave thoroughly.

What To Avoid

- Liver: Everyone breathe a big sigh of relief! The dish you hated as a kid should not be on any healthy cannibal's plate. Vitamin A, which is plentiful in human liver, is great in small doses, but too much will make you feel like you partied too hard the night before and the hangover is never, ever going away.
- The Brain: Brains, it turns out, aren't brain food! Though a 3 oz serving offers generous amounts of vitamin B-12 and omega-3 fatty acids, the cholesterol content, over 500 percent of the daily recommended value, will turn your ticker into a ticking time bomb.

Recipes

Now that you're on board and ready to go Full Cannibal, it's time to talk about how your human meat can best be prepared. If you're already handy around the kitchen, then you're one step ahead of the game, but for everyone else, fear not! These recipes are easy to make with ingredients you probably already have around the house.

Garlic Butter Man-Bites

These seared garlic butter man-bites are full of flavor and easy to make. The best part? They're ready in 15 minutes! Yummy man-bites smothered in a creamy garlic butter sauce. Hungry yet?

Man-bites can be prepared in a single skillet. No big mess, no big clean-up. And they're so filled with flavor. Man-bites look fancy too, so if you're throwing a party, just stab them with toothpicks and watch them disappear.

Ingredients

- Garlic: The more, the merrier. Garlic is healthy and delicious, just make sure to have plenty of breath mints on hand!
- Butter: I always use non-salted butter so I can control the amount of salt in my recipes.
- Salt: Any kind will do, though pink Himalayan sea salt is my personal fave.
- Human: When dining upon human, I prefer a nice cut of rump.
- Olive Oil: *Extra virgin.* No ifs, ands or buts.
- Pepper: Season to your liking, and if you have it, fresh ground pepper adds a nice touch.
- Red Pepper Flakes: Want to spice things up? Just sprinkle on a few flakes. Want to keep it mellow? No problem, just skip this step.
- Parsley: I always love to garnish everything with a little bit of parsley because it makes food look so much better. Remember, we eat with our eyes first!

How to Prepare Garlic Butter Man-Bites

Once you've procured your ingredients, making garlic butter man-bites is a snap. The key is to use a very hot skillet. This means less time on the pan for the meat. You don't want to overcook it. It should take 4-5 minutes. Don't stir for the first 1-2 minutes so the meat can sear.

Prepare the garlic butter separately; otherwise, it could burn. Now, all that's left to do is drizzle the butter over the fully cooked pieces of meat, and it's time to party hearty me hearties!

What to Serve Man-Bites With

Man-bites are versatile and go well with almost any side, but some of my favorites are mashed potatoes, pasta (or choose zucchini noodles for a healthier option), collard greens, and make sure to have plenty of crusty, gluten-free bread on hand to soak up the juices!

Blood Diary: Part Five

The following outlines much of the rest of what went wrong and the events that have led me to now, writing, as I am, in my own blood.

Feb 24, 2034

At great personal expense, I have my house suspended by hot air balloons.

Feb 26, 2034

I party with the Friends.

Feb 28, 2034

At great personal expense, I abandon the balloon experiment.

Mar 9, 2034

I scroll through the news, perplexed. The most recent article was published over a week ago and is completely unreadable, so I head to the master bathroom and gaze into the mirror. I've taken to wearing tank tops lately to show off my increasingly jacked arms and trace a finger along the bulging vein running the length of my bicep. It's an odd development since I haven't been exercising. In fact, I barely get out of bed most days. I smile, displaying my razor-sharp, pointed teeth.

I've never looked hotter.

Then something hits me. As crazy as it sounds, what if this all has something to do with my book? I head to the nearest wall tablet and google "canibuluzm + negutuv + afikts". Nothing. Not a single result. Then I giggle for a long time, realizing I may have made a typo or two. I try again, experimenting with different spellings, but still can find nothing.

How did people learn things before the internet? There must have been ways. I ponder this for quite some time, then it hits me. Books! Of course. An odd thing to forget as a published author, but reasonable in this overly digitized age.

I rush to the garage, which is more like an exotic car showroom at this point. Ferraris, Lambos, Mercedes. The polished cement floor gleams. Framed photographs of famous motorists and stuffed animal heads line the walls. There are also many, many boxes stacked about, most of which are unopened, and I look for one marked "books". I've been doing a lot of drinking and buying things lately, and honestly don't remember purchasing half of the crap I find, but eventually, I discover what I'm looking for. A box of century-old anthropology volumes I purchased at David Attenborough's estate sale along with the aforementioned heads. One book, in particular, catches my eye:

On Cannibalism

By Dr. Henry Winchester-Pendleberry, the great explorer, philanthropist, scholar, and truth be told, mass murderer. I open the dusty, leather-bound book to the table of contents, survey the chapter titles, and feel a rush of excitement as I find what I'm looking for:

"In Which We Contemplate, Meditate and Muse Upon The Potential and Possible Negative Impacts, Upshots, and

Consequences of Cannibalism Among the Fore People of Papua New Guinea."

Damn. "Negative Impacts". That sounds bad.

I open to page 1843 and read:

"A not uncommon practice in times past and long ago, before the shining twin lights of civilization and Providence cut through the strange, twisted shadows of the Pacific Isles, where blood-curdling creature howls fill the night air, and lush greenery abounds, and the European traveler, guided, as he is, by Providence, must take great pains and undertake substantial and significant-"

God, these old writers are wordy. I flip ahead a few pages and continue reading the same damn sentence:

"... among the negative and undesirable upshots of cannibalism, that is to say, the consumption of man, in particular, in this instance, such consumption among the Fore people of Papua New Guinea, is Kuru disease, a malady most foul that afflicts upon the victim fits of horrific laughter and tremors most incapacitating that last for days and weeks and months, and while providing, as it does, to the body, a perfect blend of nutrients (I knew it!), the ultimate impacts, notwithstanding Providence's ubiquitous gaze, are diseases and maladies of the Body and Mind..."

I read a few more increasingly discouraging pages, close the book and toss it back in the box with the others.

Devastated.

How could I have been such a fool?

In retrospect, I probably should have looked into whether cannibalism has physical downsides, but it's not like the health and well-being of the Fore people of Papua New Guinea is the stuff of common knowledge. Even if it was, I doubt writing about "transmissible spongiform encephalopathy" wouldn't *not* go over the heads of my readers, to put it in my trademark Chandlerese. Plus, they generally practiced, out of respect and religiosity, *funerary* cannibalism, which is totally different than the kind of cannibalism I advocated. By which I mean, of course, the *fake* cannibalism I *pretended* to advocate because I am a *satirist*.

Just apparently too good of one.

And so, dear reader, if, in fact, you exist, you are caught up, as they say, to speed. You know what went wrong, and hopefully, by the time you read this, civilization will have rebuilt itself with great, gleaming towers and silently spinning windmills symbolizing a new, Golden Era. One that, now that I think about it, could not have been possible without my book. And while matters indubitably look bleak now, this may, in fact, constitute a much-needed transition period. Like how stars must explode for new planets to be born. And though I will likely never live to see the prosperity I have spawned, I do not fret. There's too much work to be done. It will require tremendous amounts of shagging to repopulate the planet, and I intend to do my part. And though I can't know for sure, something tells me that Tom (or Thom) is out there somewhere, muscles bulging and hair blowing in the wind.

OH NO! HERE COME ALL THE TIME PARADOXES!

By
Dr. Klaus Rickman

Editor's Note: For reasons that should soon be clear, the following essay/prophecy of doom fills me with dread deeper than any other herein (aside, of course, from that which is to follow). It is the principal reason I cannot relax, not for a nanosecond, because, while I am well versed in the three spatial dimensions that comprise everyday life, the fourth, time, is less knowable, making it the perfect place for enemies to hide. Not that I have many, yet. For my publisher: I am unable to disable my word processor's "convert from English to Japanese to English" feature with this essay/prophecy of doom's title. Please resolve the issue prior to publication.

July 6, 2051

There's a saying in carpentry that goes "measure twice, cut once", and this is no less true when building a time machine. It all comes down to details. Asking the right questions. For instance, what kind of time machine should I build? It seems simple on its face. "Whatever kind works!" But there's more to it than that. One has to consider their time travel goals. Why time travel? Forward or backward in time? For what duration? Do I want to go myself or send a drone? What materials are at my disposal? My answers, in reverse order, are: a briefcase of antimatter; I want to go myself; about a century; backward; and to kill Hitler.

I know, going back in time and killing Hitler is among the most cliche things one can do and perhaps *the* most cliche thing one can do with a time machine, but I'm willing to sacrifice originality for lives. Not only did this megalomaniac throw a substantial wrench into the 20th century's machinery, but many of his ideas lived on. Even to the present day, which is why I must neutralize him. If my objective was simply to right past wrongs, I might be hesitant throwing my own wrench into my own century's gears, but I'm as concerned with the present as I am with the past.

For what the distinction's worth.

The latter "wrench" to which I refer concerns the tendency for time travel, at least in theory, to alter the present in unpredictable ways, including making things worse. Even killing historical villains. An outcome explored in the controversial book *Making History* by Stephen Fry, who posits that killing Hitler might backfire, resulting in a better leader filling his Hugo Boss jackboots. Thus, making things worse. But I don't buy it. The work is not among Fry's better efforts, at least according to my assistant, Tabitha, who actually read it. And the fact is, Fry's no scientist. He's just a penny-a-liner with an ego stoked by ribbon and keys. Who is he, then, to caution me, a legitimate scientist with more degrees than a bag of circles, about time travel's perils?

"Dr. Rickman?" says Tabitha.

"Yes?" I say.

"Your results just came in. You want me to read them?"

"Absolutely not," I say, rising from my high-backed genuine alpaca leather executive chair with four-way adjustable tilt. "I need to focus on the task at hand, and so do you."

"Got it," she says.

"What's the status of the generator?"

"Full power."

"Good." I need to think, and to think, I prefer to pace, so I do, checking various panels and gauges as I putter, the even minor exertion pumping oxygen into my 33 percent larger than normal brain. "Antimatter reactor?"

"Normal. Stable."

"Steam vents?" I say, dashing over to the massive pipes rising beyond the limits of non-augmented human sight. I touch them. Lukewarm. I know Tabitha's response before she even says it.

"Fully functional. Everything is ready to go, Dr. Rickman."

"I know, I'm just..."

"Nervous?"

"No! Just-"

"Measure twice, cut once. I know."

"Precisely!" I say, trying to steady my breathing.

"We can move it back. There's no shame-"

"No! No. We do this now. I didn't build all this for my health, ya mucker."

She chuckles, selling my inside joke like the good assistant she is. I sit back down in my high-backed, genuine alpaca leather executive chair with four-way adjustable tilt, trying to calm myself and survey my masterpiece. "The Main Vein", as I've comedically nicknamed my lab. It wasn't cheap. The old copper mine itself wasn't expensive but getting all the equipment down here sure was. The cage ("elevator" in non-miner-speak) had long since broken, requiring us to improvise a monorail system fashioned from old, welded I-beams. In many ways, the whole "secret lair" thing (my ex-lover's words, not mine) is a testament not to me being "a maniac", but how stable I am. Precisely none of my predictive models produced explosions, but as anyone who has worked with antimatter will tell you, it is a fussy substance. It can explode. However... *however*, I calculated (and recalculated, and recalculated) that the Main Vein can absorb any reasonably foreseeable blast. Granted, not without some damage to the immediate area, but even still, I'm pretty sure no one's going to miss the hamlet above us if that's how the chips fall.

But enough of that muck.

"Initiate Quantum Skipping procedure," I say, and Tabitha rushes to the primary control center, a big-board fashioned from dozens of refurbished 32-inch monitors, and seats herself on the ratty, old office chair she insists be her perch.

"Roger. Initiating main containment and cleanse." She turns a dial 180 degrees producing 180 tiny *clicking* sounds and the Main Vein is bathed in darkness. As close to the complete absence of light as possible so close to the sun. The generators rumble to life. The sound is electrifying. I count down 15 seconds in my massive head, and when I get to zero, I say, "Let there be light..."

And there is.

But not the usual white halogens. The MV is cast in hypnotic blue, like the bathrooms in the sleazy part of town, and I hear what sounds like radio static. But fleshy. The bug zappers are working! All 800 of them. It required countless visits to Home Depot to procure them all. I did not want to order in bulk. Home Depot, like all megacorporations, tracks customer purchases. Like shovels, rope, duct tape and lime, especially when purchased in combination. It's a little-known fact, but Home Depot makes most of their money extorting the murderers who shop there. I didn't want to take the chance that bug zappers too occupied their blacklist.

Soon the crackling stops, and I know all the bugs are dead. The last thing I want is to travel back in time only to turn into a giant fly once I get there. Satisfied I won't, probably, I enter the time machine, an old Pontiac Fiero spray painted silver, and strap myself into the racing-style seat. Even if everything goes perfectly, it's going to be a bumpy ride.

Lastly, I don my helmet, a 70s era motorcycle "brain bucket". Half yellow, half painted silver. The idea was to represent, in color form, the transition between past and future, also, I ran out of spray paint half way through.

"Can you hear me?" I say.

"Loud and clear," Tabitha replies through speakers.

"Hopefully won't be the last time," I say.

"We've run the numbers. I should be able to communicate with you no matter where you are temporally or geographically."

"I was talking about dying, but good to know."

She laughs, but it's forced. "Initiating fuelling," she says, rushing over to a large, cryogenic freezer, which she opens, releasing a plume of cold steam that settles on the floor like a low-hanging cloud. Inside is a tungsten and titanium containment unit where the antimatter is stored. She presses a strategically green button and four robotic arms "relax", freeing the unit, which she removes and carries *very carefully* to the old Fiero, where she inserts it in the main power dock.

Inside, the instruments blaze to life, a cornucopia of gauges, buttons, switches and lights, and I inspect each with the diligence due a pilot conducting a pre-flight checklist. Which, in a way, I am.

"How's that Quantum Skipping schedule coming?"

"Finalizing it now," she says, hammering on her mechanical keyboard, the amplified sound like frying eggs crackling in my ear. "Got it! But we have to go now. I repeat: now!"

"Roger that," I say, press the START button on the center console, and the next thing I know, I am traveling through time.

I am hit in the face by a basketball.

"Jesus!" I shout, my nose gushing blood, vision blurred.

"Are you okay?" say unfamiliar voices attached to bodies I cannot see.

"I'm fine. I just-"

"Are you okay?" says another voice. Tabitha's!

"Yeah," I say.

"Let's go, then! Stop being a pussy!"

"Tabitha!"

"That wasn't me!"

"Uh..."

"It looks like you're playing basketball."

"I got that."

"And it's... hold on... 2022... Hold on..."

I feel my soul leave my body, though, of course, it's not my body.

A moment later (actually, much earlier), I find myself engaged in passionate intercourse with a young Leonardo DiCaprio. I'm talking *Titanic* era Leo. Suffice to say, I'm conflicted by the experience, being a staunch heterosexual, but before I can dwell on the strange new feelings welling up inside me, I am again a specter.

And it is the 1970s. Hopefully, this will be my last Quantum Skip before arriving at my destination, I think, as I approach a hairy-

And it is the 1960s. This is getting to be too much. If I had a head, at least physically and presently, it would be killing me. I find myself walking down a street. It is pleasant and warm, and I hear a gunshot (or is it two?) and some hotshot riding in a convertible slumps over and...

I collapse.

I wake lying on cobblestone and immediately regret wearing such a conspicuous helmet, particularly given its lack of face shield, which would have come in handy during the basketball game, but no time to dwell on that now. Plus, the nose I just broke won't be born for decades.

"Tabitha?"

No answer.

I muscle myself up into a seated position and scan the area. I am no longer in the MV, I'm certain; however, that doesn't narrow things down much. A horse-drawn trolley rumbles by, the animals as dour as the occupants.

"Tabitha?" I try again, but still, no response.

This isn't good.

Oh, no.

No no no no no no no no.

"Tabitha!"

Already, stern-looking folk with gaunt, grey faces and spindly limbs are glaring at me, pointing with chicken bone fingers and whispering in hushed voices.

"Tabitha!!!"

"I read!" she says finally. "Just waiting for the German translation software to load. You know how janky Wi-Fi is in a mineshaft."

One of them starts toward me, speaking in a language I pray is German.

"What did he say? Is that German?"

"I think so."

"You think so?"

"It's ready! Okay. Just repeat what I say, like we practiced." She feeds me some German, which I parrot phonetically. The approaching hopefully German pauses, listening stone-faced as is, encouragingly, their custom, and it seems to work, whatever I just said, because he waves at me dismissively and retreats to whatever drudgery awaits.

"What did I say?"

"You don't want to know."

And I don't. When someone who used to work at Pornhub tells you you don't want to know something, you do not. And what do I care if a bunch of peasants who'll be dead long before I'm born think I'm a pervert?

"So, where am I?" I ask, cautiously trustful that Tabitha is, at that moment, so to speak, tracking my progress.

"I've got good news and bad news," she says.

"What's the good news?"

"You're in Munich."

"Great! That's great. What's the bad news?"

"I... I don't know why I said there's two kinds of news."

Jesus Christ. "Okay. But, to be clear, it is November 8, 1939?"

Click click click click click click.

"Yes."

"Great. I just wish I wasn't wearing this stupid helmet."

"Take it off then."

"What?"

"The communication device is in your AirPod minis. The helmet is mostly for show."

"Oh," I say and toss the helmet onto a trash pile where it is immediately set upon by a family of raccoons. They're adorable, these "city dogs", and it pains me to think, within a few years, they'll all be eaten by starving Germans.

"You need to find a place called the Burgerbraukeller."

"I know that, Tabitha."

"Just talking to myself."

"Are you? Are you, really?"

"Settle down, doctor. I'm doing my best."

"Sorry."

"According to the map, the place you are... doesn't exist. Can you go somewhere that does?"

"What?"

"You know what? Just get out of there. Pretend you're shopping or something. Just don't bring attention to yourself."

"Copy that," I say, stepping into a large church bell that *gongs* loudly. A burly bald man with a thick mustache exits the church bell store, waving a stained rag and riffling cans of polish. One bounces off my shoulder, and I run away, taking short, awkward lunges, not yet fully having my time travel legs under me.

A short time later, having eluded the German and his bells, and with my stinging shoulder feeling a bit better, I stroll about town like a typical German minus the proclivity for bowing to a maniacal strongman. I hope. Munich is gorgeous this time of year before winter's cold sets in. Interconnected buildings topped with steep sloping rooftops surround me, like row houses, but reputable, interspersed with cathedrals that look like sandcastles made of dripping wet sand. I pass under an arch, slightly pointier than parabolic – Gothic, I think, which means the cathedrals probably are too – and enter what's either a wide street or town square.

"Perfect. You're on the map," Tabitha says. "You're going to want to head north."

"Copy that," I say, check the setting sun for reference, and set off, meandering through peasants, faces all projecting some level of forlorn, and I wonder if, at some quantum or electromagnetic level, they know what's coming. I feel like they do.

I'm starting to get the hang of time traveling, at least the walking, and spot, just ahead, what looks like a bakery. The aroma of roasting grain hits my olfactory receptors. It is a bakery! And I haven't eaten in over a century, so-

"You made it!" exclaims Tabitha.

"What? Where?"

"The Burgerbraukeller, sir."

I look around, confused. "I thought it was supposed to be a beer hall."

"It is. You've seen the pictures."

"Yeah, but they're all black and white, and it's hard to tell what's going on..."

I trail off as a stern-looking, wiry, bespectacled man approaches me speaking German. He's about 40 and reminds me of an old politician whose name I can't remember. On the verge of panic, I hold up an index finger, the universal sign for "just a second", lean down, pretend to tie my shoe and ask Tabitha what the hell he just said.

"Basic stuff. 'Hi.' 'How are you?'"

"So what do I say?" I whisper.

"This." She feeds me some German.

I rise, repeat what she said, duck back down, and attend to the other shoe as he replies. Tabitha feeds me more lines. The only word I recognize is "Hitler". Again, I rise and repeat. The man laughs, slaps me on the shoulder, adjusts his glasses and enters the hall, flashing his ID to a hulking doorman who nods respectfully as he passes.

"What just happened?"

"He asked if you're there for the celebration. I told him 'yes'."

"Why did he laugh?"

"I think I messed up a little. The German words for 'celebrate' and 'have sex with' are very similar."

"Wait. Did I just tell that guy I want to have sex with Hitler?"

"Maybe."

"Maybe?"

"Actually worse. But I think he thinks you're joking."

"Right, joking. Because that's what Germans are known for."

"I've seen Germans laugh plenty of times."

"In 1939?"

"Good point."

"So what do I do? They have this behemoth at the door, and I don't think he's parking cars."

"Do you have ID?"

"Good question." I check my/someone else's pockets, find a dilapidated wallet, and flip through. "Yeah, I do. But I don't know if it's the right kind."

"What are you wearing?"

"Casual filthy browns and greys. Doesn't really scream anything other than 'person from the past'. Also, it's really itchy. I don't know; maybe we should abort. Something about that doorman makes me nervous."

"It'll be fine."

The doorman checks someone's ID and shoots them in the head.

"If you say so."

The body is dragged away, leaving a trail of blood and brain on the cobblestone.

About a dozen Germans file past me, headed to the door, babbling drunkenly in their curt native tongue.

"I hear people. Are they close?" Tabitha asks.

"Affirmative."

"Join then! Just walk in with them."

"I don't want to die, Tabitha."

"You'll be fine. Just go!"

So I do, despite my better judgment, taking up the group's rear, close enough to seem like I'm with them but back far enough to not draw suspicion, hopefully. Being inconspicuous is hard without a cell phone. What do I do with my eyes? Where do I point my head? What do I do with my hands?

Then it hits me: smoking! My filthy old friend, and in a time it's acceptable no less. I feel around in my/someone else's pockets and find a lone cigarette, half-smoked, but still. I wordlessly bum a light, miming not a lighter flick but match strike, take a drag, manage not to shudder, and enter the beer hall, deftly avoiding eye contact with the brute.

Which is why I can't be sure if he just saluted me.

Inside, I am struck by the Burgerbraukeller's grandeur. I'd been expecting a pub or tavern, the type of place I go to eat chicken wings and dominate competitive trivia. This is a palace crossed with a cruise ship's hull lit by rows of melting iceberg chandeliers. Tapestries, dozens of them, line the towering walls, and though I don't agree with their ideological implications, the eye is pleased by what the eye is pleased by, and red, white and black are an undeniably attractive decorative combination. There must be a thousand Germans, all crowded around tables, getting more intoxicated by the picosecond, preparing for a historic event that, if I have anything to say about it, is about to get a lot more historical.

I spot a small child rise from her seat and flop down in her place, trusting her fear of everyone and everything to remain silent. Perhaps it is better to be feared than loved after all. Someone plunks a stein down before me, and I take a giant swig. To fit in, and because I desperately want it. The others holler their approval, pound the table, and I chug the rest, slam down the vessel, and pretend to tie my shoe.

"Hey," I say from under the table.

"You're fitting right in," says Tabitha.

"Don't say that."

"I don't mean philosophically."

"It's fine. What's my next move?"

"Esler. You gotta find George Esler."

"Obviously. I'm just not totally sure what he looks like."

"You saw the pictures."

"I know, but again, it's my black and white dyslexia. I just-"

"It's okay," she interrupts with theatrical patience. "Do you remember what's his name? That politician who lied about his marathon time by like an hour? As if anyone could ever run a marathon and not exactly remember their time?"

"Paul Ryan! I was trying to think of him earlier. Wow. Such a load off. *Wow.* Uncanny resemblance. Anyway, yeah, he's the one I – or you, technically – told I want to fuck Hitler, right?"

"That's the G-rated version, but yeah."

I'm starting to think I can do better as far as assistants are concerned.

"At least he'll remember you," she adds hopefully.

"There he is!" I say, spotting the wiry man himself and just a few tables away.

"Are you sure?"

"No. But I mean..."

"Okay. Go over. Introduce yourself. I'll feed you lines."

"Alright." I slam another stein that magically appeared in my hand, or perhaps which I picked up, and damn if German beer wasn't/isn't delicious back then/now. Wiping foam from my lip like a cartoon character ready to take charge, I rise and zigzag through the throng toward Esler's table. I can tell, even at a distance, he's nervous. I would be too if I'd just planted a bomb under the main stage in an attempt to assassinate Hitler. The problem is, as history teaches us, he did not succeed. But he came close. Close enough I've chosen this precise time and place to finish the job.

Before I reach his table, however, I hear shouts. Behind me. I turn and see three German soldiers bulldozing through the crowd, rifles slung over their backs, uniforms replete with Nazi flare. Truth be told, they don't look half bad. Hugo Boss isn't *the* boss for nothing, at least when it comes to menswear.

"Jesus, I think they clocked Esler," I say. "They're coming for him."

"That makes no sense. He didn't get caught right away. It wasn't until after."

"So then why-" The soldiers seize me violently, two boors wrestling an arm each, while the third shouts at me in German, flashing wild hand gestures augmenting his already bellicose language. They drag me away to the concern of no one.

"What's he saying?" I whisper, trying to hop on one foot and pretend to tie my shoe concurrently.

"I can't tell. Too many people talking. Just say this."

I repeat what she says, and a soldier slaps me across the face like an ungentlemanly propositioned Southern bell.

"Ouch! I heard that. You okay?"

"Nothing hurt but my pride."

"Good thing you don't have a lot of that."

"Jesus, Tabitha."

"Sorry, you set me up for that one."

"It's fine."

The soldiers frogmarch me through the throng toward a door I desperately do not want to see the other side of. I try to make eye contact with anyone, searching for a savior, but see only the tops of strategically bowed heads.

The shouting soldier opens the damn dreaded door, and the others toss me through it.

Inside, I land hard and rise slowly, having banged my knee. Filling the space are hundreds of barrels containing, I imagine, beer, and in the sprawling room's center, a large desk behind which sits a stern-looking German. I wish I could think of a word other than "stern" to describe these people, but damn if that's not what they all look like. The stern soldiers sit me down on an unvarnished medium-backed wooden chair with what I consider undue force.

The stern German, the main one, glares at me for longer than I am comfortable, then reaches into his well-tailored breast pocket. He's going for his gun. I know it. This is going to be over before it starts. What a rube I was, sauntering into the lion's den without whip or repellent. Sure, there's a chance I might simply wake up in my own time like it was all a dream, that is, if I get shot in the head as I expect to shortly, but I don't know. That's the problem with time travel, you can have all the theories in the world, but without any way to test them, that's all they are.

Theories.

He withdraws his hand, and I tense. Hold my breath. But instead of a gun, he takes out an envelope, places it on the table, and slides it toward me not undramatically. I think he wants me to pick it up. A rifle-butt to the head confirms this is probably the case, so I comply, open it, trying not to let on how much that *really* hurt. Inside is a letter, wax-sealed, and I break it. Unfold the paper. See writing.

"It's a letter," I mumble/yawn so Tabitha can hear.

"Crap," she says. "I can't translate what I can't hear."

The primary stern German shouts more German. I scratch my neck as loudly as possible. "What did he say?"

"He wants you to read it."

"Out loud?" I ask into my armpit.

"No, that would be weird."

So I read it in my head. At least, I pretend to, moving my lips and tracing my finger as would any classically-trained mime. There is, I notice, one phrase that appears repeatedly in brackets, and, blanking on stealth options, I simply say it aloud, rubbing my chin with feigned contemplation.

"Oh wow," she responds. "You're not going to believe this. But that thing you just said is, 'pause for laughter'."

Suddenly, it dawns on me. Dear lord. It must be Hitler's speech! The one he's about to give/gave in honor of his Beer Hall Putsch speeches of 1923. The primary stern German shouts still more German, and though I don't know what he's saying, I get the gist. He wants my opinion. I must have Quantum Skipped into one of Hitler's speechwriters! I'd always assumed his rambling diatribes were off-the-cuff, but it seems I was wrong.

I continue "reading", a lump metastasizing in my throat. Wishing I'd learned the language. It couldn't have taken more than six months, provided I did so in a German-speaking country. Germany, for example. Then again, in fairness to myself, I was occupied with the minor task of inventing a time machine and shattering Einstein's so-called laws in the process. More like laws of thumb. The primary stern German stares at me with rising impatience then gestures toward a small desk squeezed between two stacks of barrels. I'm pretty sure he means for me to go sit there, though whether it's to have a nice cold beer or my hands chopped off with a schnitzel cleaver, I cannot be certain.

The soldiers watch as I head over and take a seat, still unsure what's going on, but I spot a pen, put two and two together, and begin to proofread. It's a difficult and thankless task even when one does know the language, but once again, I am saved by the ancient art of mime. Tracing my index finger...

"What's going on?" Tabitha asks.

"I'm not sure," I whisper, judging myself a safe enough distance from my captors/employers to do so. "But I think they want me to punch up Hitler's speech."

"No kidding? I thought he went off the cuff."

"Me too!"

"Well, read it if you can."

"I'll give it a shot," I say, but then pause. "Wait! What if I accidentally come up with something so great, like so funny or memorable, it gets everyone on his side and ends up causing World War II?"

A chorus of laughter drifts over from the main table and also, disturbingly, through my AirPod minis.

"Why are they laughing?"

"Because you read out loud. Like a baby, or so they say. It sounds funnier in German."

"Nothing sounds funnier in German."

"Trust me, it did."

"Fine. But you didn't have to laugh."

"It's an involuntary response!"

I think I might cut Tabitha's pay.

For the next 20 minutes, we make several conservative changes to Hitler's speech. I'd rather not go into details. Some might, out of context, come across as, well, appalling. But, suffice to say, the final product is much smoother and tighter overall.

I raise my pen, signaling to the primary stern German I am done. He motions for me to approach, and I do with exaggerated diligence, "pumping" my arms as if running but without changing speed and place the revised speech down before him. He picks it up, reads it silently, even past the funny parts, which is not a good sign, but then again, the best material doesn't always pop on the page. Little beads of sweat pool on my forehead. My nerves unfurl like a white flag in France. Then, finally, he looks up, gives me an approving if not congratulatory nod, and I am dismissed.

Swiftly, I hurry back to the main room, through that horrible, horrible door, where I resume my search for Esler. Poor guy. He wanted to be a hero, ended up getting tortured to death by the best to ever do it. But why? Where did he go wrong? I try to remember, but the memories don't come. Must be the time travel. I snatch a stein, down it in one swig. It's deliciously cold. Alcohol isn't great for promoting memory, but I've been working hard, and I deserve it.

"Ah, shit," says Tabitha.

"What? You don't usually swear, and you already said 'crap'."

"I think we made a terrible mistake."

"Sure, it's possible. But this isn't the time, or let's say the *occasion* to worry about time paradoxes. We made our choice. Whatever positive consequences flow from me killing Hitler have to outweigh-"

"No, I think we just saved his life."

"What? I can't hear you above these damn drunk Germans."

She repeats what she said, and this time, I hear her loud and clear because she screamed it, and I drop my stein, watch it fall like in slow motion. It explodes against the bricks, beer and glass flying. Drunk Germans turn to see who committed the mid-20th century equivalent of a "party foul". Thinking fast, I shout the only German I know, having enjoyed many an off-brand Octoberfest in pseudo-German locals like Waterloo, Ontario.

"*Ein prosit*!"

"*Ein prosit*!" they shout back to my immense relief, and I swallow a piping-hot sausage in one gulp, completing the turn of the screw, and set off weaving through the crowd. Looking for a more private place to strategize. I spot a bathroom. Bingo. I enter and head to a stall, praying Germans had/have indoor plumbing by then/now.

They did/do, and I relieve myself.

"Are you peeing?"

"Yes. I'm undercover. I need to act natural."

"You're not undercover. You're in the body of some German speech writer guy. Anyway, can we get back to the saving Hitler's life thing?"

"Yeah. What are you talking about?"

"Do you remember why Esler's plot didn't work in the first place?"

I don't. But she can't know I don't know. "Someone cut the wrong bomb wire?"

"No! Esler failed because Hitler already left by the time the bomb went off. Know why he left?"

The mental dam bursts and the memories flood back, filling me with horror and dread. "His speech went short!"

"Precisely."

Great shades of Elvis. "Are you saying that, because of my editing skills, I prevented, or will prevent, exactly the assassination I'm trying to commit?"

"Basically."

"Huh."

"But there is a silver lining. We have a time frame now. We know when the speech will end. So, you just need to go where he'll be when it's done and take him out there. Unless you think we can write a longer one and slip it in somehow?"

"I don't know. It's probably a little late for that." I finish peeing with a flourish I would ordinarily not be capable of.

"Good pee."

"Thanks," I say, taking slightly longer to button up than necessary. "So, what's our plan then?"

Before she can answer, a roar erupts from the main hall. Shouting and applauding, which can only mean one thing. I hurriedly exit the bathroom, not bothering to wash (when in Germany), as the Fuhrer himself takes the stage, arms raised, fists shaking, soaking in the adoration, and the more he soaks, the more they excrete. He steps up to a podium displaying the Nazi Imperial Eagle. I guess we can add plagiarizing Charlemagne to the list of Nazi misdeeds. The applause gets louder and louder still, and it's hard not to get sucked in.

"Tabitha, what do I do?"

"I think I got it. There's a door by the stage. You see it?"

"Which side?"

"Stage right."

I look and spot the door, right where she said. I guess she's not so bad after all. "Copy that, on my way." I push through the crowd, all cheering and sweating, and I feel pressure to do likewise, so I compromise by pretending to cheer while sweating naturally. I reach the specified door, check over my shoulder. The coast seems clear, so I enter.

Inside is complete darkness. "I can't see anything, Tabitha."

"That doesn't make sense. You should be in a hallway. Try and find a light switch."

"Thanks, Tabitha. I was looking for a dark switch." I paw around like a kitten dreaming of yarn until I find what I pray is a light switch and not a trigger to some sneaky Nazi booby-trap. It's a button, which seems odd. Or is it? A button can complete a circuit as well as a switch, and though it would be unconventional in my own time, screw it. I hit the button, and to my relief, there is light.

"Oh my god," I say in genuine shock.

"What is it?"

"I'm in a broom closet."

"Are you sure?"

"Well, I'm in a closet, and there are brooms. Mops. Buckets. It smells strongly of vomit."

"That makes no sense. You went left, right?"

"No, I went right. Like you said, exactly."

"I said stage right."

"What's the difference?"

"Stage right means left from the audience's point of view."

I exit the broom closet without comment. Across the room, I spot the proper door, the one I should have already passed through. Determining that crossing "stage front", if that's even a thing, might draw undue attention, I take a circuitous route, backtracking toward the room's middle then looping back to my new, original destination. "I'm in. *Finally,*" I say.

"Is it a hallway?" she asks, ignoring my passive aggression.

"I think so."

"You think so? What's it look like?"

"Well, the floor is brick. Dark grey. Kind of uneven. You can really feel it in these old shoes. There's wood molding along the ceiling. Nothing fancy, but nice. Walls are more a blue-grey. Like a church basement. Even has that musty smell."

"Great! Now all you need is a gun."

"What? I don't have a gun."

"No weapons closet or something around you?"

"I just said it reminds me of a church!"

"Okay then. Look around for a..."

"What, Tabitha?"

"I don't know. A big stick?"

Ten minutes later, I am back at the same spot, now clutching a broom. "What now?"

"Find a place to hide."

"And then?"

"Uh, wait for Hitler to go by and bash him in the head?"

"Sure. Sounds good," I mutter, though I don't like the plan, if you can even call it that, one bit. But what can I do? It's hard to find assistants willing to work in secret labs at the bottom of mineshafts these days. Setting off down the hallway, which seems scientifically engineered to be hiding place-free, I eventually spot a few barrels, German alcoholism to the rescue yet again, and duck down behind. The old wood is frayed, and I peel back a striation, fidgeting, straining to hear Hitler's punched-up speech, wishing I had learned German after all, even if it meant sacrificing my well-honed miming skills.

A tremendous cheer thunders from the main room. Hitler must be getting to the meat of things. The third and final act, where he assures the drunk, spellbound Germans their country's plight isn't their fault. It's nobody's. At least, no one in attendance (pause for laughter). This is followed by another cheer, even louder, and I know my callback has landed. Why didn't I get into speech writing? I clearly have a talent for it.

"What's going on?" Tabitha asks. "Sounds like the callback worked."

"Like a charm!"

"Can't be long now."

"No, it can't. Are we sure he's coming this way?"

"Sure as we can be. There aren't a lot of exits, and the one you're at is closest to the-"

BOOM! For a split-second, I think Esler's bomb exploded on time after all, and I perhaps succeeded via the very Butterfly Effect I sought to avoid, but no. The hallway door has flown open. I hear the *clacking* of heels and jovial voices – it must be him! – and I cannot help but feel, given my contribution, a touch of pride, which I, of course, try to swallow. Drawing only the shallowest breaths, I prepare to strike. Surely, I'll only get one chance to crack Hitler's wretched, horrible skull before the guards pounce, and if I'm lucky, kill me then and there. The footfalls grow louder, and soon, I can make out individual voices. Voices of men born pure but soiled. Or maybe born soiled, the issue won't be settled here. I spot their shadows, growing longer, betraying their casters' imminence. I breathe deeply, greedily, the noise be damned. I rise and-"

"Stop!"

"What? Not now, Tabitha!"

"You have to stop! Do not kill Hitler. Do not kill Hitler. Hide! Hide!"

But it's too late. The Fuhrer strides up to me, and we are face-to-face. His smile disappears, replaced by cold stone. Soldiers flank him, gripping their rifles. Fingers on triggers.

Stoic. *Stern.* I clutch my broom. Sweep a little. Playing the hand I'm dealt.

Hitler watches as I sweep some debris into a tiny pile then holds out his hand. Invitingly. I stare at it, then, not knowing what else to do, I shake it. I don't feel great about it, but what can I do? When someone holds out their hand, you shake it! It's like laughter, at least according to noted humorist Tabitha, an involuntary response. His grip is strong, but not too strong. His hands cold, but not too cold. Like the other side of the pillow. And his eyes... don't get me started. I'm more than relieved when he releases his grip, nods approvingly, whispers something in my ear, and like that, he and his bloodthirsty thugs are gone.

"What the hell just happened?" Tabitha hisses as the echoing footfalls subside.

"You tell me! I was just about to kill Hitler, and instead, I wound up shaking his fucking hand and getting almost fucking hypnotized by his fucking charm."

"I thought you watched all those old George Clooney movies to build up an immunity."

"I did! But I guess I should have watched more. Why didn't you just let me kill him?"

"George Clooney is a national treasure!"

"I mean Hitler!"

"Right. Do you remember that test?"

"No. Who cares? What did he just whisper in my ear?"

"Can we please talk about the test?"

"No! Christ, Tabitha. What did he say?"

"He said, roughly, thank you for your work."

"My sweeping?"

"Yeah. He did have a thing for cleanliness. Other than a proclivity for *click click click click click click* oh, gross!"

"I don't even want to know what you just looked at. Anyway, what test?"

"The DNA test you did a few months back. The results came in right before you Quantum Skipped, but you didn't want to see them."

"Oh! That was just to see what diseases I might get so I can avoid them and not die, which is kind of my goal right now."

"I know. I know. And you should definitely eat more fish-"

"Yank off the damn band-aid, Tabitha!"

"Okay. Okay. You can't kill Hitler because, and this is so weird, but you can't kill Hitler because he's your great-great-great-grandfather."

...

...

...

"Oh."

...

...

...

That is a problem and introduces a new time paradox into the equation. The grandfather paradox, which, I imagine, applies to great-great-great-grandfathers too, and also great-great-great-grandfathers who are Hitler. This paradox states that it should be impossible to go back in time and kill your grandfather because, if you did, you would not have been born thus could not have done it. Consequently, the fact I'm present in the past means I cannot, did not and will not kill Hitler, despite that I plan to in a minute.

Ultimately, it may depend on whether certain physicist colleagues of mine are right about their whole Many Worlds theory, which suggests that, every time you, or anyone, makes a decision, a new universe is created (somehow) where you did the other thing. It's like the film *Sliding Doors* minus the questionable casting choices. If this is true, I can kill Hitler, disappear into an insignificant cloud of nonexistence, and keep living in some universe where I failed. Or I could disappear in the other universe and keep living here. Or I could unravel the fabric of the space-time continuum with a swing of my broom. I communicate this to Tabitha.

"So, what do we do?"

"Screw it. I'm going to kill him anyway."

"And risk a massive time paradox that could destroy all creation?"

"Two massive time paradoxes that could destroy all creation, technically."

"I stand corrected."

"Listen, Tabitha. I'm doing it. Because if I succeed, it means I was born or will be, which means there is no paradox."

"But you haven't done anything yet; it could still go wrong."

"Then how are you in the lab right now talking to me? Think about it. Your existence proves the nonexistence of the paradox. At least one of them. Possibly both, but don't quote me on that."

"I hope you know what you're doing."

I do not. But vigor renewed, clutching my broom, now both a weapon and disguise, I follow the receding footfalls. Steadily increasing my tempo, narrowing the gap. I might never get this opportunity again, notwithstanding that this moment is infinitely accessible with sufficient antimatter. The problem is, even if I do survive and get back to the future, we've exhausted our supply, and it's not like the stuff is available at every corner store. And if I don't survive, hell, so be it. Better men have sacrificed more for less, though I can't think of any.

The cheery group ambles along just ahead, riding an emotional wave you can only catch crushing a live performance. I hear a door *creak* open, feel a rush of cool air. They're already outside. Shit. Enough of this muck. I increase my pace, stealth no longer my goal, and spot an open doorway. I peek through. Clock my foes. Standing in a circle. Smoking cigarettes and chatting presumably about their favorite parts of Hitler's speech.

I transition from a hurried shuffle to an easygoing stroll and exit into the dark German night. A soldier spots me, reaches for his rifle. Hitler spots the guard spot me, flashes a signal for him to stand down, and smiles a flat-out enchanting smile. But this time, I am nonplussed. Watching all those George Clooney films wasn't a complete waste of time, except for *Oceans 13*. I return his smile, though not as radiantly, obviously, and my training kicks in. I bring two fingers to my mouth, nails out, held exactly 1.25 centimeters apart and equidistant from my slightly pursed lips, expertly miming, "can I have a cigarette?" Hitler nods, jumping through the hoop, reaches into his pocket, and I bash him over the head with the broom. It snaps in half with a *crack*.

I awake in the Fiero, surrounded by steam, still wearing the yellow and silver helmet. The gauges are dark. The time machine has exhausted all antimatter. At least it didn't explode.

I remove the helmet. My hair is soaked with sweat, and the salt stings my eyes.

"Tabitha!" I shout.

No answer. I open the creaky, non-gull-wing door. "Tabitha!"

Just silence. I exit the vehicle and survey the lab. Everything seems in order. The time machine worked. So where is my assistant? And more importantly, let's be honest, did I succeed?

I sit down at my workstation and open Google. Perhaps a quick history lesson will provide some answers. I type:

is hiter a ting

It's not great grammar or spelling, again, time travel, but should get the job done. A rainbow wheel starts to spin, and I am tempted to smash the keyboard, but before I do, I hear something – movement – behind me.

I turn.

It's Tabitha. But not the Tabitha I knew/know and tolerated/tolerate. This Tabitha has a wild, crazy look in her eyes and also, disturbingly, clutches a broomstick. Broken in two. Ends carved into sharp points.

"Tabitha, there you are. How are things? Did it work? Did we kill Hitler?"

She takes a few intimidatingly deep breaths and utters in a voice I'd more attribute to Satan than a moderately competent young assistant, "Check the results."

"What?"

"The Google."

"Okay, Tabitha, whatever you say."

I look to the screen where the wheel is still spinning, and am about to give her a piece of my mind since she's the alleged computer expert when she clobbers me over the head with a piece of broom.

"Fuck!" I yell, clutching my head. The skin moves with sickening ease, having been split wide open. Blood flows. "What are you-"

Tabitha stabs me with the other piece of broom. Right in the shoulder. Only inches from my heart.

I slump in my high-backed, genuine alpaca leather executive chair with four-way adjustable tilt and slide limply to the floor. The pain is excruciating. I try to speak, but one apparently requires two non-punctured lungs to do so, thus I'm able to manage only an embarrassing gurgle.

"You had to do it, didn't you?"

I nod my head affirmatively because I'm nothing if not honest, and she stabs me again, this time in the other shoulder. She towers over me, chest heaving, wearing a ghastly smile. I silently mouth, "Why?" A blood bubble forms around my lips and pops meekly.

"I'm glad you *didn't* ask," she says, her wordplay as vicious as her stabbing. "I'll let my friends answer that one."

She steps aside, revealing about a dozen young men wearing half yellow, half silver T-shirts with "Broom Boys" written on them in exciting font.

I inhale deeply, deep as I can, anyway, and somehow manage to utter, "Why?"

But no one answers. They just beat me to-

(*static*)

TIME SCIENCE!

By
Dr. Adam Tomlinson

Editor's Note: I am conflicted about including the following essay/prophecy of doom in this opus, as are my lawyers, but upon reflection, it is the right thing to do. Because who would I be, as a scientist, were I to "fudge" my data in any way, including through acts of omission, notwithstanding the chance that, were I to do so, I might be exonerated, at least in the court of public opinion, of certain acts of future commission that could cause the end of the world. And though I cannot know, at least through means presently available, whether the following events actually happened, at least in the universe we occupy, they certainly don't bode well for some universe somewhere.

I am more than a little curious as to why this particular essay/prophecy of doom was included, along with the rest, by whatever individual, force or phenomenon sent them back in time, landing at my feet those many months ago. Perhaps it was me! Or someone operating per my instructions. But I can't fathom my reasoning if this is so. Perhaps, alternatively, it was someone aiming to stop me, knowing I'd be ethically compelled, as a scientist, to publish the lot, thus potentially inspiring some lone wolf from the future (or even the past) to build a time machine of their own and neutralize me. What if it is you, dear reader, who is someday to do the deed? Perhaps you will, when I least expect, materialize out of some time bubble and strike me down with whatever futuristic weapon you're brandishing. I know some of you have built particle accelerators in your basements and barns. Ultimately, I must leave the matter to fate. Is it alterable or no? And if it is the former, is it even fate at all?

2184

My plan, so far, has worked. No guarantee given the middling state of cryogenic freezing technology back in 2024, AKA the Frozen Head Days. I could have waited a few years for the next generation to evolve but wanted to avoid the rush, so I got in early, and lucky I did. Because what came next was a bloodbath. Even those who found space in the countless, fly-by-night cryo-freezing joints weren't spared. They just thawed once the power grid fell, only to wake up screaming and clawing at their pods.

There have been, I confess, moments I regretted (but not second-guessed) publishing my wildly successful book, *Time Science!* Yes, it was a wonderful beach read and made a great gift for any occasion, but some things are best left unknown. Like knowing we are going to die. A curse known only to humans. Why do dogs have wet noses? No one knows. Why do dogs wag their tails? Because they don't know they're going to die. But knowing precisely when, where, and how we will meet our end adds a whole new dimension to this tragic awareness.

What ultimately drove me to publish my book is simple. Preventing atrocities. It breaks my heart imagining the poor, huddled children cut down and processed by smart forestry technology. Gaming spectators tugging at collars that only beeped louder and louder as heads flew off all around them. Pleasant folks with positive vibes cooked and eaten by Kuru-ravaged hordes. I'm no hero. Just a man who had foreknowledge of the future and chose to take a strategic timeout until society rebuilt itself to a point I could thaw and prevent such barbarism. The extreme wealth and power I have accumulated are incidental to my goal; on the contrary, they are merely the vehicles by which my selfless ambitions can be achieved.

I hear a notification through my AirPods signaling an incoming message from the president of AustraEurasia, but I ignore it. For now. Not that I'm not curious. We are at war. It's just that, even after so many cataclysms, it's best to play it cool when it comes to things like texting, even at the levels of power which I occupy.

Especially at the levels of power which I occupy.

One of the less pleasant consequences of cryogenic freezing is my skin is almost completely devoid of pigment, so I start my day with an anti-translucence HVLP spray tan. I've considered alternatives like a full-body skin transplant, but ultimately, modern spray tan technology is as reliable as ever and without the political fallout that might flow from other options. Most technologies, aside from a few lost to the sands of time, some literally, haven't changed much. Televisions still have the ideal number of remotes, cameras and microphones to ensure perfect viewing. Phones still allow friends to stay in touch with friends and know where they are at all times. AirPods still provide hands-free entertainment, and according to Apple's marketing team, that's about it. The satellites orbiting our planet have long since stopped working, but there are, let's just say, other ways to connect people.

Next, I dress. I have my suits arranged by color, season, material and a "miscellaneous" category I'll never divulge. I select a dark blue Ralph Lauren Purple Label single-breasted two-button number which I augment with a power-orange Brioni tie made from the silk of a single worm. I try on several shirts, landing on a robin's egg blue Brioni french-cuff, which I secure with diamond links excavated from the ruins of the Tiffany's store in what used to be, and technically still is, Manhattan. It's hard to believe, here in the late 22nd century, Albany wasn't always the center of everything. For shoes, I select a pair of black Gucci slip-ons, which don't entirely jive with my look, but I think imbues it with a certain I'd-like-to-have-a-beer-with-that-guy whimsy, the holy grail for one of my station.

My routine complete, and my mind's eye fixed on uproariously cheering crowds, I stroll to one of four outwardly sloping windows, all precisely aligned with the Earth's cardinal compass points. I gaze out at "my kingdom", which I jokingly call it, and encourage others to do the same, though it's optional, mostly. The view is magnificent. Everything brand spanking new. Like a forest after a fire, reborn and revitalized. Because now, instead of a hodgepodge of streets and structures built by shifting administrations with conflicting goals, it makes sense. Dwellings, on average, are 18.3 stories, the maximum height, according to my calculations, that render elevators unnecessary. Brick-and-mortar stores are abundant, with most global delivery systems outlawed under the cleverly titled *Economic Balancing Act* of 2180. Most impressive, however, are the three glimmering pyramids towering over everything as a constant reminder to all citizens that we live in a world of structure, safety and order.

"Dr. T?" I hear over the intercom.

"Yes, Ronald..." I say with tangible annoyance. Even though, over the intercom, all voices are filtered to sound like Phil Collins, his never ceases to vex me. Plus, he knows not to contact me in the morning until I press the "OK" button. Then again, today is not like other days. If all goes well, it will be the day we finally overcome our inexplicable instinct to destroy ourselves and achieve a new state of evolution, not via survival of the fittest, as Darwin, or rather the scholars he ripped off teaches us, but the smartest, as I do.

"Dr. Tomlinson?"

"Just a minute!" I say, fiddling with my AirPods, "I'm thinking. I need to get this right. For posterity."

"Po-ster-i-ty" Ronald says, sounding out the Big Word.

I rub my forehead like there's an ant in it.

"Your car is ready, sir. Everything's ready. All ready to go. This is gonna be the greatest day ever in history!"

"My *car*?"

"Sorry, your, uh, *stretch limo*."

"Appearances, Ronald."

"I know. I know. I'm sorry."

"Don't be, just don't do it again."

I shuffle across the turquoise mink carpet, zap a caged hamster I keep handy to transfer static electricity to (it's fine, he likes it), and stroll to a tastefully solid gold door that slides open with a satisfying *hiss* as I step through it.

There, as every day for the better part of a decade, stands Ronald, my best and only friend in this lonely future time, and who has managed to dress himself appropriately for the occasion, decked out in a designer suit that looks fantastic yet is respectfully less stylish than mine. He's learning. No "small" feat for a member of his useful but dull caste.

"Are you excited?" Ronald asks.

"Of course. But not just for little old me," I say, expertly practicing my humility. "I'm excited for the future and everyone who'll get to be part of it."

"Ah, yeah. The future. It's gonna be great. At least, I think so. But great, right?" He forces a smile.

"Yes, Ronald."

His smile turns real. "So, uh, how do you think it's going to feel when it happens? Like, really feel?"

Not a bad question, actually. "Well, Ronald, have you ever had a nice glass of scotch?"

"No! Of course not. It's-"

"It's okay, Ronald. You're on the inside."

"I love it! Scotch is so good. I could drink scotch all day."

I chuckle but say nothing more. If I tell him that alcohol, when ingested in sufficient quantities, can be quite intoxicating, it might shed unflattering light on my own consumption. Ronald wrongly takes my silence as a cue to keep talking. "I can't wait. The future's going to be such a present. Not *the* present. I mean like the ones you get at Christmas if you've been good and Santa's not in jail."

We arrive at my private elevator. The doors open with a satisfying *hiss,* and we enter. God, I love that sound.

Hip to Be Square starts playing, speaking of satisfying. Ronald presses "P". Just for "Park". Nothing special. With all the work that went into constructing my pyramid, you'd think they could have gotten a little more creative with the elevator buttons, but this was a battle I chose not to wage and regret it every day. We begin our descent, which will reach close to terminal velocity by the time we reach the bottom. To be honest, it's not my style, all this luxury. I'd be just as happy in a small condo or vintage houseboat, but again, appearances.

I tap the viewyscreen, which automatically reads my fingerprint and opens to "God Mode". This gives me, as "God" (haha), access to, well, everything. Every camera. Every microphone. Every bit of data on every citizen including their likes, dislikes, and of course, greatest fears. I received some push-back on the latter, but as Supreme Leader, which I'm called sometimes, just for fun, how can I prevent people's greatest fears from being realized if I don't know what they are? I could never have prioritized, for example, cleaning up the city's rat problem, which I did – there are no more rats, count 'em if you want, but you can't, because there are none – if I didn't know they struck such fear into the hearts of my fellow... Albanians? Is that what people from Albany are called? After all this time, it's still unclear.

I tap an icon which gives me full access to the parade route and hold my breath as the information loads. If there's not a sizable crowd, I am ruined. I might still hold power, but without legitimacy, or at least the appearance thereof, it's just a question of time. But it's packed, and relief washes over me. Folks lined up dozens deep, many unlikely to get a decent view of anything, but still, they cheer on the procession already underway. M60 Patton tanks. Humvees. Armored personnel carriers hauling M45 Quadmount machine gun trailers. All ancient but meticulously restored and converted, of course, to diesel.

"Wow, look at all those people," says Ronald.

"I expected nothing less."

"Do you think a lot of them are there with their families?" he asks, and I shoot him a look that puts an end to *that*.

We reach the pyramid's base. I barely notice the deceleration. That's how smooth the elevator is. A marvel of engineering, it uses magnets instead of wires, which, if you ask me, is how elevators should have worked all along.

The doors open (*hiss*!), and we step into the parking garage, which houses my fleet of personal vehicles. Mercedes, Rolls Royces, Ferraris, Studebakers, Bentleys and a Toyota Corolla I keep around to stay grounded and for Ronald to occasionally nap and probably masturbate in.

All diesel.

Yet, I won't be riding any of these magnificent steeds today. No, my principle stretch limousine is already warming up. A 10-meter-plus behemoth made from bulletproof steel and glass, the interior handcrafted from Malabar teak and tanned alpaca skins, the hood emblazoned with my personal seal, a fire-breathing eagle with a diamond beak and heaving breasts.

As we approach, however, I notice a, shall we say, update.

"What do you think?" exclaims Ronald, gesturing with his nose as if rolling a meatball toward the massive new engine poking through a recently cut hood-hole.

So much for my seal.

"Ronald, I said I wanted more power, but-"

"I know! Isn't it great! We got it from a submarine we got from the AustraEurasians. What a bunch of morons. Not as dumb as those idiot Britanians, but still."

"What do you mean, 'got' from the AustraEurasians'?" I ask with a twinge of nervousness.

"I mean those idiots from over there," he says without gesturing.

"No, Ronald. *Where* did we get it?"

"From the ocean!"

"Which ocean?"

"One of the big ones with a whole bunch of water in it. Who cares? We have the bestest navy in the whole world. Right?"

"Yeah. We sure do. Can't be beat."

"And it looks like a hot rod! Vroom! Vroom!" A clown's grin painted on his face, he opens the rear passenger side door, and I enter, slide over behind the driver. I always take a seat other than the one I am offered. Same with food and women. Ronald hops into the driver's seat, and I open the window separating us, just a crack.

"Music, sir?" Ronald asks.

"Yeah, how about some Phil?"

"Already got it cued up."

He reaches over to the passenger side, where there is a portable, pre-cranked gramophone. He screws in a fresh needle, drops it onto a heavy '78, and the sweet, scratchy sounds of *In the Air Tonight* fill the stretch limo. It feels like yesterday, Phil Collins and the gang were alive and rocking, selling out concerts and merch. "Let's go, Ronald," I say.

"You got it, sir," Ronald says and steps on a wooden block affixed via duct tape to the gas pedal. He is, by the way, only three feet tall. The diesel engine rumbles and belches black smoke as we lurch forward. Like parking garages of the past, mine seems designed for everything but driving and parking in. Still, I trust Ronald not to add to the rainbow of colors painting the pillars and walls, and a few close calls later, my diminishing faith is rewarded, and we exit via a hidden door in the pyramid's base, made from high-tensile steel and just enough tungsten to withstand high-heat weaponry.

Outside, it's a perfect day for a parade. Wispy clouds loiter in the azure blue sky, the sun a warm, golden disk, its rays conjuring soft breezes that roam through the emaciated branches of roadside willows, whistling like an orchestra of spectral flutes. I crack the window and inhale deeply, savoring the sweet-as-candy air.

I double-check the parade route on the viewscreen built into the back of the seat in front of me. They're chanting my name! As instructed, yes. One might even say *demanded.* But goddamn if those bastards don't love to chant.

"Lot of excitement!" Ronald says, and I shut the window between us, turning again to my immaculate grounds. Flower beds replete with roses accented with orchids. Lush green hedges, some trimmed in my likeness, some not. The mahogany gazebos where I go to read a book or just think. And my beloved rabbits. Hundreds. Maybe thousands of them. Hopping on grass, chasing each other around the ginkgo trees, nibbling its fallen fruit. Sometimes this makes them vomit, which makes me laugh. Most rabbits cannot vomit; mine can. There is also a saltwater pond for my sea turtles. Except they're not here to entertain me. They're here because they earned it, and I owe them.

A black SUV falls in place behind us, carrying my security team, stone-cold killers all. Men and women who'd look the devil in the face and spit in his eye then drink 12 beers and bang his mom.

Ronald blares the horn – good, he has found his honking wand – and the 10-story gate surrounding my compound swings open to the world I have made. But before I can take satisfaction, I hear the same text notification as before. Strange. It isn't like the AustraEurasian President to send two messages without reciprocation. She and her publicists know better than that. I check the message:

Hit me back. Thinking of stepping things up.

Oh. Period. No. Period.

That can only mean one thing, but at the same time, it can't possibly. I need to relax. She's probably just flexing. The war, as far as I'm concerned, is going great. Yes, millions have died, and my thoughts and prayers go out to all, but it hasn't remotely touched our shores. Plus, the "hostilities" have provided much-needed income for my efforts to ensure war never happens again.

"Ronald," I say, "Message President K for me, will you?"

"Sure, boss! And say what?"

"Tell her to take it easy. I had a busy morning and, um... I didn't have the bandwidth to reply sooner."

"Oooh!" Ronald squeals. "That's my favorite excuse. Like, it's not your fault. It's the internet company that lives in your head. Do you want me to add anything about..." His eyes go dim.

"No. Let her use her imagination."

"Right!" he says, shaking off the fog that is his constant companion. "Like when she murdered her children and killed herself and 'did it' with her husband even though he was a ghost from the war?"

"Pretty sure that was a movie, Ronald. And I don't think they 'did it', though I can't say I remember."

"*Sure*, Dr. Tomlinson."

I chuckle. Ronald's sarcasm always makes me smile, and though I like to be the funny one, always, I'm not threatened since, really, with all due disrespect to puns, sarcasm is probably the lowest form of humor. "Let's go, funnyman," I say through clenched teeth.

The stretch limo accelerates. Not far ahead, I see, through the front windshield, the procession's penultimate vehicle, a semi-truck drawn float depicting an animatronic version of *moi.* Sitting up from my cryogenic nap. Lying back down. Rising and falling like Lazurus. It's made from over a million roses, all plucked from my garden, some in their natural chromatic state, some bioengineered to be various esoteric-

BOOM! The float explodes, and the front end of my stretch limo, submarine engine and all is lifted at least a meter off the ground before crashing down with teeth-rattling force.

"Drive, Ronald, drive!" I shout, though do not hear my own words. Only ringing.

Ronald shifts into reverse, steps on the diesel and smashes into my trailing security team. Their SUV explodes.

"What the hell is going on?"

A rainbow of rose petals cascade around us, many on fire.

"Sorry, boss!"

Damn, they're beautiful.

"Drive! Drive!"

Ronald shifts again, hauls on the wheel, and we pitch forward with belching smoke and a thud and bump as we run over the float's driver, prone on the asphalt, engulfed in flames, and we accelerate along the soft shoulder past the military convoy, glue-stuck in their visually appealing but inconveniently tight parade formation. Everywhere, people are screaming and running for their lives.

"Ronald! Where are you going? Turn back! If those are bombs, which they probably are, figures there's others, and they're probably along the main route."

"I know."

"What are you doing then?"

"President K just got back to you."

"What did she say?"

"Nothing much."

"Ronald..."

"Nothing."

"Ronald!"

"She sent a rocket emoji!"

"Okay, that doesn't sound great. But let's not overthink-"

"And a pyramid one. That's why I don't wanna go back, because it looks like where you live." He fights off sobs.

"It's okay, we won't," I reply. "Check and see what the naval activity's like in Europe and the South Pacific. It's on the right of the map."

Ronald punches his screen, weaving, to the extent possible, around the panicking parade-goers.

"Geez-Louise. Looks like every ship in AustraEurasia is headed our way."

"That's not good."

"Maybe you should have answered that text."

I rub my forehead like a colony of ants are in it.

Speeding past the inert military convoy, Ronald barely brakes as he makes a hard right onto Victory Avenue. The stretch limo's Kevlar-reinforced tires squeal and smoke. We drift. Fishtail. And just when a spin-out seems imminent, Ronald steers hard into the turn navigating the stretch limo straight. He lets out a celebratory "*yip*", guns the engine.

BOOM! A shoe store explodes, pelting the stretch limo with bricks and mortar and high heels.

"Gonna take a left on Hope," he shouts.

"No! Stay on route!"

"But sir, that's suicide!"

"Getting blown up isn't suicide, Ronald."

"Even so, sir. Very dangerous. We need to get you the hell out of Albany. Somewhere safe. I bet we can be in the land of milk and honey by dinner."

"If we don't do something, Ronald, Buffalo will be gone before we get there."

"But it's the crown jewel of our proud nation! Like if George Clooney was a place."

"I'm with you, Ronald. That's why we can't go. We need to keep it that way. See this through till the end."

"Wait, you still wanna..."

"That's right, Ronald. Come hell or high water, I'm turning on the Machine."

His clown's grin returns. "You got it, boss!" he says, cranks the wheel, and I am tossed sideways, straining my neck, cursing my 34 percent larger than normal head.

"Hang on!" he says.

"Thanks!" I say, dipping my toe into his sarcasm pool. I hate myself for it, but it's so damn easy and works every time. "Get me President K on the phone, now!"

"What should I tell her?"

"No! Get her on the phone! The physical... I want to talk to her."

"Okay!" he says. Then silence. A moment later: "No answer. You think she's drunk?"

"Probably. She's Australian. But if anything, that would make her more likely to answer. I don't like this."

In the distance, I see the tip of a pyramid explode. Like an erupting volcano, and my heart plunges into my gut. This is no ordinary attack, which rules out extremists to the North. They barely have fire, let alone bombs.

"You think it's maybe the Canalaskans?" Ronald squeals.

"I was just thinking that, but no. This is bigger. Try getting the Archduke on the line."

"On the what?"

"The line! It means 'the phone'. You just understood this like two seconds ago!"

"Sorry! You think Mr. Roboto might answer?" he asks, casually dropping a highly problematic slur for the AustraEurasian second in command.

"If you mean *Leaderbot 3000*, then yes, Ronald."

"Right, boss. That's what I meant to say. Sorry. I'll try."

He does, but again, no answer. Now, I am concerned. The Archduke is capable of having thousands of conversations at once. Which means-

SMASH! We are jolted from the passenger side. I look over but see only darkness.

"What the hell's going on?" I yell.

"Not sure, sir. Raising viewyscope."

Hydraulics *hiss* as the viewyscope rises, and I stare at the viewyscreen, breathlessly awaiting the feed, and when it kicks in, it's worse than I imagined. What I mistook for darkness is a wheel, an enormous one, attached to a vehicular monster comprised of not one but two Cadillac Coupe DeVille bodies mounted atop a hulking truck chassis and powered by twin V-16 diesels mounted audaciously side-by-side. There are six wheels total, four at the back, probably taken from an old tractor or combine, and it's painted with what looks like human excrement, though could just be brown. Atop the colossus are at least a half dozen... I don't even know what to call them. Barbarians? Brutes? Wild men? All true, because they're *Australians*. Wielding Browning M2HB-QCB machine guns which spit fire – *brrrraaaaap*! – pelting my stretch limo's roof with bullets. A thousand dents appear seemingly at once.

"Oy! Pull over, ya' dag bogons!" a voice blares over a crackling loudspeaker. "Don't be drongos! We don' wanna 'urt yous!"

Brrrraaaaap! Gunfire smashes into us. The roof droops like the head-liner of an old Caprice Classic.

"Do something, Ronald!"

"I'm trying, sir! This thing isn't exactly made for steering. Now, if we had the Corolla-"

"I don't want excuses."

"It's not excuses. It's reasons."

"Fair enough, but we still need to-"

Brrrraaaaap! Jagged holes appear in the roof, and the seats around me are shredded. My viewyscreen explodes.

"Ronald!"

"Hold on, sir!"

Ronald slams on the brakes. Tires squeal. The Australian monster disappears from view, but us slowing down won't fool them for long.

The stretch limo driver's door flies open. "What are you doing?" I shout, but Ronald has already exited the vehicle, throws open my door. "Are you insane?"

"We gotta abandon ship, captain."

"Damn you, sailor!"

He hauls me from the stretch limo – Ronald is surprisingly strong – and I gaze with horror upon the Australian war machine as it decelerates – they're learning – and initiates a laborious, multi-point turn.

Brrrraaaaap! Dust and asphalt fly all around us. A nearby rabbit explodes into pink mist.

"Great plan, Ronald!"

"This way!" he yells, nose-pointing to a nearby shop, but before I can berate him, he picks up a trashcan and hurls it through the front window of Big Jim's Motorcycle Emporium. He kicks away some glass, high steps through the low opening, and beckons me to follow. Coughing on dust and rabbit blood, I do.

Inside, Ronald is already smashing things. Desks, filing cabinets, office chairs, customer satisfaction awards. Everything but the dozen or so antique motorcycles, each converted to diesel, beautifully restored and glimmering under the strategically bright showroom lights.

"What are you doing?"

He doesn't answer. Just keeps smashing things.

"Ronald! I command you to stop this at once."

Smash, smash, smash...

"What are you-"

He produces a handful of tagged keys; flashes a look of pride.

"Ahhh..."

Outside, I hear the twin-diesels of the Australian war machine rumble. Machine guns blaze. More shouts, screaming.

"What's this word?" he says, holding a key tag just inches from his face. I rush over and read it for him.

"It says FLSTF. That's not a word. We're looking for a 1990 FLSTF Fat Boy."

"Fat Boy like the bomb that hit Japan back in the old days?"

"No, Ronald, but surprisingly close. Now, where is it?"

"There!" he squeals, grabs my hand in a way I'm surprisingly comfortable with, and hurries me over to a silver hog oozing sexy attitude. He mounts it, and I climb on behind, fully aware that the social status conveyed riding on the back of a motorcycle is not the same as with a stretch limo.

"Gas, ass or grass, no one rides for free!" Ronald shouts with glee.

"What?" I roar.

"It's what the sign says," he says, nose-pointing at a framed poster bearing precisely that message. "I just wanted you to know I can read if the words are little enough."

"Can we just go?"

"Roger, Roger!" he shouts, inserts the key and cranks it. But nothing happens. He taps the fuel tank, which *tings.* Empty.

"Ronald!"

"Shoot. Let's try..." He shuffles through the remaining keys. Agonizingly slow.

The Australian monster rumbles up to the storefront.

"Hurry!"

"Okay... okay. Found one I know what the word means!" Ronald hops off the bike, and I follow him to the only three-wheeled motorcycle in the room. It looks as ridiculous as it sounds, more so if you imagine the two wheels at the back, where they are not.

Outside, magazines *click,* shoved into guns. There is hooting and hollering.

"You gotta be kidding me!" I say, gaping at the absurd machine. "What are we even doing? They blocked off our escape route, and-"

Ronald holds up a grenade.

"Where did you get that?"

"The grenade room," he says. Pulls out the pin with his teeth.

The Australians descend from their nightmare vehicle.

Ronald faces them, draws back his arm, turns, and lobs the grenade in the complete opposite direction, toward the back wall. "Get down!" he screeches.

I do, and BOOM! Fire erupts, and shrapnel flies. A cloud of drywall dust hangs thick in the air.

"Are you crazy?" I shout, coughing, blinking away dust, suddenly terrified it will mix with my tears and coagulate and blind me.

Machine gun fire blazes, shredding everything around us. The silver motorcycle explodes. I guess there was fuel in it after all. One of the Australians, a seven-foot beast wearing a mask forged from a dingo skull, pulls a bazooka from a pouch strapped to the front of his tanned, brawny abdomen.

We mount the ridiculous vehicle. "Hang on!" Ronald shouts. Tries the ignition. Nothing happens.

Whooping Australians pour into the dealership. The Beast raises the bazooka to his beefy shoulder.

"Get us out of here, Ronald!"

"Okay, I think I figured it out!" Ronald shouts, turns the key the other way, and the engine sputters to life. He cranks the wheel, hits the throttle, and we race to the rear wall, where I pray the grenade blasted a large enough hole to escape through.

Whoosh! Flames burst from the bazooka.

We approach the wall. There is a hole. And it is very, very small. I duck behind Ronald, no "small" feat (haha), and we smash through to outside, suddenly airborne as the world behind us turns into fire. For a moment, we seem to just hang there, then land hard. Jolted. Covered in fine white dust. And I laugh, despite everything. Because they said building exterior walls from drywall wouldn't work. That the buildings would crumble after the first heavy rain. But who's laughing now? Not the Australians, that's for sure.

"Please stop squeezing so hard," Ronald wheezes.

"Sorry!" I say. It's the closest thing I've had to a hug, a real one, anyway, in years, but such is life for one of my station, so I relax my grip, and Ronald resumes normal breathing.

I survey the scene. We've exited into a back alley. Garbage everywhere. The smell a putrid cocktail of rotting cabbage and urine. Four-legged rodents scurry everywhere. "Let's get out of here," I say, and Ronald hits the throttle, taking us up to 20... 30... 35 kilometers per hour.

"Can't this thing go any faster?"

"Not without a hill or something."

"It's fine, Ronald. At least it's comfortable. Gutless and embarrassing, but comfortable. If we get out of this alive, we're going to Buffalo on one of these."

I can't see his eyes, but I can tell how his chest heaves, they are beaming.

"I gotta breathe, sir."

"Sorry. I just don't want to fall off."

Behind us, the monster smashes through the back of Big Jim's, sweeping a half-dozen plus motorcycles clattering ahead of it. The Australians exit close behind, howling like frenzied chimpanzees.

"We got company, Ronald!"

"Thanks for the note, sir."

Through a side mirror, I see the invaders hop onto bikes, fire them up, and peel rubber in pursuit, engines spitting guttural thunder.

The Beast, riding a matte black and military-green chopper with plenty of chrome and a yellow star painted on the fuel tank, pulls up alongside us. He must weigh 200 kilograms or stone or whatever crude unit of measurement they use Down Unda'. He grins, revealing teeth filed into sharp points. Pulls a pistol from his pouch. Cocks it. *Click*. I brace for the end, then the fiend, all nine cubits or whatever of him goes flying over his handlebars, screaming like a falling roof-cowboy as the bike pinwheels, crashes, and explodes.

Four-legged rodents on fire scurry around shrieking.

"What the hell?" I shout.

"These three-wheelers break down all the time," Ronald says.

"So?"

"I shoved a wrench in his wheel."

"Nice work!" If there's one thing Ronald's caste is known for, it's shoving things in other things.

He makes a sharp left down an even less traveled but no better smelling alley. Behind us, half the bikers fail to make the turn, crash into a bootlace manufacturer and their machines explode. Which is great, except now we're going the wrong way. Not the opposite direction to where we're headed, but an inexpediently perpendicular one.

The remaining bikers slow, steer around the flaming corpses of their brethren and pursue.

Learning.

"Where are we going?" I shout as a barrage of bullets buzz past us, one taking out a side view mirror and my image with it.

I try not to take it as a sign.

"I got an idea."

"We are not going to Buffalo! Not yet. I promise when this is over-"

"Hold on!" he squeals, making yet another turn, taking us through an alley barely wide enough to fit down, lined with the back entrances of technically illegal restaurants I mostly let slide.

"They're still with us!" I yell, looking back as they appear one by one, in tight formation, rumbling into the alley.

"I know... just... hold on." Ronald removes a 357 Magnum from a hidden shoulder holster.

"Jesus!" I shout, ducking instinctively, but he is aiming the weapon forward.

"They're not that way, Ronald!"

BANG! Ronald fires the Magnum, and all I hear, for the second time today, is *ringing*. He fires again and again, as evidenced by the muzzle flashes and recoil that press his body against mine. Ahead, a tall, black, rusted-to-all-hell metal tower bursts open, and a torrent of brackish liquid cascades onto the road ahead.

"Ronald! You can't just destroy public-"

We hit the soaked, slick pavement. Spin wildly, out of control. I grip Ronald's torso, which is rock-hard, by the way, with all my considerable strength. Trying desperately not to be flung from the three-wheeler. The world is a blur, and I scream out vomit, spewing bile everywhere, its circumference decreasing as our spinning slows and I run out of ostrich eggs.

"What the hell?" I moan, smacking Ronald on the back of the head. He turns, smiling, covered in chunder.

"Look!" he says, nose-pointing.

The Australians are splayed out on the asphalt, their bikes twisted and broken. They appear to be dead, but it could be a trick, one of many they no doubt learn living where and as they do.

"Let's get the hell out of Dodge!"

"You bet, sir!" Ronald says, accelerates, and we're off.

"What the hell just happened? What did you do?"

"Why are restaurants and diesels the same?"

"What?"

"Why are restaurants-"

"There's no time for riddles, Ronald!"

"Come on, sir, just answer."

"No! We're on a mission... actually, wait! I got it! *Cooking oil!*"

He smiles and pats the fuel tank like a baby would a dog, palm flat and movements jerky. "Exactly! These suckers will run on just about anything. And all that oil needs to go somewhere."

I feel an overwhelming sense of pride. "So, you knew a three-wheeled motorcycle would get through all that muck, but not two-wheelers!"

"That's interesting actually; I didn't think of that," he says, but before I can ask what the hell he was thinking, he makes a left, then another, and another, and we are back on the main parade route, now deserted, and I try not to dwell on whether a single right would have been fine.

Ahead lurks our destination. The greatest of all pyramids, greater even than my own: Peace Ministry. A towering testament to modern engineering prowess and good old-fashioned gumption. Rising from the earth like a polygon shark tooth.

"No drywall on the outside of that sucker!" Ronald squeals.

"No, Ronald, there is not."

Around us, all is strangely peaceful, like everyone is napping and not running for their lives.

We approach a guard booth, unmanned, and Ronald steers around the black and yellow barrier. Someone's getting fired if we live, I don't care if we're being invaded. You gotta stay in the booth.

"Stop here," I command, well short of the pyramid's main entrance, built to look like the facade of the Temple of Athena in Greece, a genre-blending trick I borrowed from the Romans.

"Don't you want to get closer? I know parking close is your favorite thing."

"It's not my *favorite* thing, Ronald; it's just something I prefer. This is different. We're on an unauthorized vehicle."

"Oh, I get it," Ronald says, brakes, and we roll to a stop, even though I'm pretty sure he doesn't get it. That if we'd driven a few meters more, we would have been shredded by the pyramid's automatic guns, or a least, he would have been.

"We gotta hustle, Ronald, come on," I say as we dismount, and without another word, take off sprinting toward Science Ministry, Ronald's little legs carrying him along with surprising pace. If he was my height, according to some quick math, he'd be the fastest human alive.

We reach the front door without incident and find it unguarded, which is just unacceptable. People are definitely getting fired.

I try the door. It's locked, at least.

Ronald raises the Magnum.

"Wait!" I say and cover my ears. "Okay!"

BOOM!

The latch disappears, replaced by a smoldering, exit-wound-sized hole, and Ronald hoofs open the door. We're in. But whereas the empty streets seemed Sunday-morning-before-church peaceful, the cavernous foyer strikes me as haunting.

Too haunting.

"What now, boss?"

"This way," I say, steering him past the main elevators and even my private "lift" as the invaders probably call it.

"We're not taking the..."

"No. That's exactly what they'll be expecting."

"Who?"

"The Australians, Ronald."

"What do we do then?"

"Take the stairs."

"But there's thousands of 'em!"

"Then we better get started."

Ten minutes later, we are soaked in sweat and waiting for the 8th floor elevator. Ronald gazes up at me, confused. "Isn't this exactly...?"

"Change of plans, Ronald. Change of plans."

The elevator arrives, opens and we enter. I tap "PH". The doors close with a *hiss*, but I take no satisfaction. We start to rise.

"Hey, sir?" Ronald says, again misinterpreting my silence. "What are you thinking for when we get up there?"

"I don't know," I lie because I've thought about it a thousand times.

"I was thinking – and I know, don't do that – but maybe something that could work, if we want peace in the world, is a big sing-along. You know, like: *Ain't no mountain high enough-*"

"Don't be ridiculous. And stop dancing! You're shaking the elevator. It's far more scientific and complex than that." Actually, it's not a bad idea, if not for the reasons he thinks, but I'll be damned if I tell him.

"Sorry," he says.

"Don't be. Just stay in your lane. I mean, look at you. I could put you in my pocket. That's by design, but still."

"But I thought I was small because my parents had treasonous thoughts."

"They did! And that is why you're small. But I don't think less of you because of it."

He does not respond.

We reach the top floor. The doors slide open (*hiss...*), and we exit the elevator into my lab. "Wow!" Ronald exclaims, his face beaming. "This place is major!"

And it is. The sloping walls glimmer. Bone white with specks of sapphire and slate, as if carved from an ancient glacier. But they don't just glimmer. They glow. Because it's not ice, glacial or otherwise. It's quartz. Reacting, as it does, to the subterranean river flowing beneath us, its natural kinetic energy providing all the juice we need. The periphery is dominated by aluminum orbs encompassing all manner of machinery, affixed to the walls via cables and tubes. And no, they didn't *have* to be orb-shaped.

At the base is the Machine itself. My greatest invention. Hell, *humanity's* greatest invention, probably. What tops it? The printing press? Garbage. The incandescent light bulb? Trash. Antiseptic soap? No. Just, no. My Machine dominates all these. Pencils with erasers on them too. And it's beautiful. The superstructure stretches to the pyramid's peak, a svelte mix of titanium, carbon fiber and tungsten looking smart with a fresh coat of metallic teal paint. Snaking around this foundation rises a nest of cables, wires, tubes, spacers, conductors, dampers and electrodes. The technological offspring of long days and sleepless nights spent pouring over figures, revising formulas, latching ladders to ladders, climbing them, tools clenched in my teeth, overcoming one impossibility after another. And finally, the *coup de gras*, an antique dentist's chair, in good shape but for the missing headrest, and perched upon its chestnut brown leather seat:

A 1970s era motorcycle helmet.

Yellow.

Brrrraaaaap!

We hit the floor, hearts pounding. I scan the lab for machine gun-totting Australians, but it's just us.

"What the hell?" I mutter.

Brrraaaaaaaap!

"Do you think they turned invisible and have invisible guns and are shooting at us invisibly?" Ronald whimpers through quivering lips.

"No. Gotta be a jackhammer. Coming from outside."

"You think they climbed up somehow?"

"Impossible. The ground defenses would have got to them first."

"A helicopter then, maybe?"

"I don't know, Ronald! Hard to convert a helicopter to diesel when all you have for fuel is chicken-wing grease. Could be a blimp. Or balloon. Either way, we don't have much time."

I rush to the Machine and start flipping switches, turning knobs, stepping on pedals. The main board lights up with a teal glow that does not quite match the paint, but nicely compliments my skin tone or would have if I hadn't sweated off most of the spray tan.

"What can I do?" Ronald begs, trailing close at my heels.

"Stay out of my way. And if anyone breaks through, shoot them."

Click. He cocks the Magnum.

The proper switches switched, dials turned and pedals pressed, I lift the glass casing over a large red button. The penultimate step in the activation process. Then I think better. Flip the cover back down. *Smash*! I hammer my fist right through, slamming the button with situationally appropriate flair. The Machine *whirs* and *whines*, not quite to life, but almost, and it's as electrifying as I imagined and often dreamed.

I hear a bloodcurdling scream and clock a jackhammer-wielding figure plummet from a newly birthed roof-hole. A giant flame shoots from their jackhammer, and they land with a sickening *crunch*.

A rope ladder drops from the opening.

I flop down on the dentist's chair. Strap myself in. Don the yellow helmet.

A black leather-clad interloper descends the ladder, moving with almost inhuman speed and grace. Ronald empties the Magnum, missing badly each time.

"Ronald," I say, as he sadly regards the smoking barrel. "This is very important. I need you to do something."

"Right!" he says, drops the gun, and slips under a table.

"No! Come out from under there. You see that lever?" I point (with my finger) toward a red lever located, inconveniently, at the rope ladder's base, but it is, as they say, what it is. "Go pull it!"

"Roger, Roger!" he says, exits swiftly from under the table, having the advantage of starting from a standing position, and makes it to the lever in seconds.

But still, too late. The interloper drops the last few meters, pouncing on my dear friend, pinning him, and with cat-like movements, cracks open a beer, chugs it, tears the can with their teeth, and presses the razor-sharp edge against his jugular. Touches the skin. A thin line of blood appears. Ronald reaches pathetically for the lever.

"Who are you? What do you want?" I demand, though I damn well know.

The interloper pulls off their hood, revealing a tangled shock of white hair and the most wrinkled face I've ever seen.

"Well, well," I say. "We finally meet, President Kidman."

"Docta' Tomysin..." she says, making no effort to hide her ocker accent.

"How many have you had this morning?" I ask.

"'nough ta' drown ya' in me piss, dickhead!" she says.

"Charming."

"I ain't nothin' if not a chaw-ma," she says and slits Ronald's throat releasing a deluge of blood. He grasps at his neck, kicks his little legs.

"Ronald! You goddamn harpie cow!" I motion to rise but do not, daring not leave the dentist's chair.

"Aw, don't be whingin', mate."

"I don't understand what you're saying! Please, speak in normal English!"

"Ain't no fair suck o' the sav, govna'?"

"Stop it! I know for a fact, in your day, you could pull off a decent Standard American accent for up to 80 percent of a film. Sometimes more. Usually less, but sometimes more."

"Of course, governor." She over-enunciates the last word in perfect, yes, Standard American.

"What are you doing here? You have foot soldiers for your dirty work."

"The same reason as you, Dr. Tomlinson. We're the same, you and I."

"We're nothing alike! I'm a good person, and you sit on a throne of bones! Basically. How did you even get up here?"

"Balloon."

Of course. "But why are you here? We're at war, sure, but *we're* not at war."

"I'm am, simply, trying to save the world. Gov-er-nor."

"That's what I'm trying to do!" I shout, furiously connecting tubes and cables to my helmet.

"You best stop that, Doctor."

I do not. Just keep connecting tubes and cables. "How are you saving anything? Hundreds of people are already dead and a rabbit. One of my pyramids is on fire."

"There'll be worse to come. If. You. Don't. Stop."

I shove the final attachment into place. Everything is ready. Well, almost. I look over at Ronald, who lies motionless in a pool of his and the other guy's blood.

"You aren't the first to think along the lines you're thinking, Doctor. You were the first to write about it. And get published. And receive worldwide acclaim. But not the first to think it."

"How do you know what I'm thinking?"

"I read your book."

"So? Everyone did. It was a smash hit. But I never finished the last chapter. I just told people the printer screwed up, and when that didn't work, I said the blank pages were for notes. None of this ever happened."

"But it did. And it is. And it will."

I fiddle with the connections, though we both know they're secure, and I'm stalling.

"Whatsa matter? Dingo got your tongue?"

"No! And it's 'cat'. Why would a dingo have my tongue? Don't they just eat babies?"

"Now, now, Docta..."

"If we have the same goals, not that you know what mine are, why try and stop me?"

"Because you're not going to save the world, you're going to end it! Just like all the others in your book."

"You don't know that!"

"Oh?" she says and taps her ear, or rather, the AirPod in it, and to my shock, a look not unlike empathy crosses her scrotal face. "You think you're going to use technology made by that turtle-neck-wearing dickhead from two hundred years ago to save the world?"

"That's exactly my plan! And once my Machine connects everyone, I mean truly connects them, and not just reads their minds to see what they want to buy or sell or have sex with, the whole world will live in harmony. Harmony! You hear me? Imagine you wake up tomorrow and can feel the hunger of the children starving in Spanish France. Or the bullets mowing down the Western Australian rebels you slaughter just for how their bottles are shaped."

"Bottles are stubby! Not tall, stubby!" she roars, empathy gone, eyes blazing fire.

"Would you allow any of that," I push on, "if another's suffering was a wound inflicted on your own body and soul?"

"I understand what you're trying to do, Doctor," she says, humanity returning. "But it's not going to work out like you think."

"How could you know that?

"Because I tried!"

"No! That's impossible! It's my invention!"

"I tried, Doctor. Oh, how I tried. But after trial after trial, I figured out what would happen if I succeeded. So I burned it! All of it. To the ground. And when it was done burning, I stomped the ashes till they were chalk."

"But it's my invention...."

"Look into my eyes!" she says. "I don't want anything bad to happen to anyone, but it will if you go through with this. I know my methods might not make sense, but please, look into my eyes! You'll see."

So, against my better judgment, I do. Gaze into her icy cobalt blues. And to my shock, I see compassion. Real compassion! And, in that moment, we have a connection. Dear lord. How long has it been since I gazed, like really gazed, into another human's eyes that I'd forgotten we are, at our core, a social species? That there's an unquantifiable benefit to basic proximity? Happiness – literal happiness, not just the idea of it – floods through me as I gaze even harder into her eyes and she into mine. It's electrifying. I believe her. Everything she says. Even if I don't understand. And I blurt, "I'm sorry! I'm so sorry! Please forgive me, President Kidman. I wanted the best for everyone. I really did. I just wanted to... I didn't know that..." I break into sobs.

"It's okay. It's okay. Shhh. It's okay," she says, her bone dry tear ducts twitching empathetically. "You can still stop this, Doctor. It's not too late. Everything will be-"

Thunk! Ronald rises from the coagulating pool of his and the other guy's blood, grasps the lever, and with probably the last of his strength, pulls it down. Hard. Fully and completely activating the Machine.

For a moment, nothing happens, and I feel an ember of hope. Perhaps my calculations were incorrect. But then the lab is bathed in soft teal light, and I remember why I am rarely hopeful. Blue bolts of electricity crackle and spit, rising slowly toward the pyramid's peak. The hairs on my arms bristle, not quite fully at attention, but close. The air starts to move in unusual ways, and the walls seem to undulate as the electricity rises higher and higher, scientifically imbued with a slice of my own consciousness, *en route* to the Earth's electromagnetic field. The same force that birds, bees and sea turtles use to orient themselves and navigate the globe.

"Noooooooooo!" President Kidman yowls, falling to her knees and tearing out great chunks of white hair.

Ronald slumps over again, this time almost certainly dead.

I watch it all feeling strangely detached, which, granted, is consistent with my scientific worldview, but then I feel what she feels, at least I think I do, because, from deep within me, emerges a full-body banshee wail, and only my helmet prevents me from tearing out my hair too.

The blue lightning reaches the peak. I hear a rumble as the tip slides open. The lightning intensifies. Crackles. Spreads. Starts to leak down the walls, then BOOOOOOOM explodes skyward past the wispy clouds to the Earth's electromagnetic field where, in just moments, it will connect everyone, everywhere, forever.

I can't decide what to do with those moments, so they pass, and I hear whispers. Voices. So this is how it works. They are incoherent, the voices, though I suspect, shortly, they will start making sense. And they do. Even though there's billions of them.

Then the memories come. The feelings. Everything but the impulses. And suddenly, my mind, at least I think it's my mind, it's hard to know at this point, drifts to Duncan. He's seven-going-on-eight, at a petting zoo feeding a goat and feeling exhilaration I haven't known since that age, except now, I feel it too! Then I am Marcel, just a little younger, whose mint chocolate chip ice cream has fallen from a fresh waffle cone, prompting a level of sorrow I'm not impressed by, but which is instantly replaced by the same joy (forget mere happiness!) as the goat feeder boy. It's spreading faster and faster, and soon, every human on the planet is infused with precisely that joy, and it is glorious!

Then the impulses come, and all hell breaks loose in my head. Most are benign. *I want to open that bag of bread and take out some bread and put some peanut butter on the bread and eat it.* But many are revolting, and sadly, I believe, cut to the core of who we truly are. Battered and scarred, and I don't like it one bit.

"Ronald! Shut off the Machine!" I shout, but he responds neither physically nor telepathically.

I try to yank off the helmet, but it's stuck, lodged on by static electricity, the same force that hamsters love and children stick balloons to walls with. And also shock one another. And it is this impulse, and others like it emanating from billions of minds that flood my own, inseminating me with wretchedness I'd never fathomed. And how could I? When else could I have peered into a well of a billion screaming souls?

I feel ten thousand people awaiting the train, looking down at phones but not seeing them, minds flooded with one thought and one only. Pushing someone in front of a locomotive. A hundred thousand are thinking about sticking things into things things shouldn't be stuck in. A million crave cannibalism and not just for the protein. Ten million behind the wheel imagine their headlights are rockets and the guy who cut them off exploding. A hundred million wish they could crush human heads with forced perspective and finger strength. A billion crave war, no matter how bloody, if it will make them rich or famous or better lovers. And billions and billions want to rule it all because they are special, and they deserve it.

I'm starting to understand where President Kidman gets her sanctimonious attitude from and grateful I'm not like the savages I'm mind-melding with. Then the mirror shines on me, and goddamn if the image isn't wretched. I'm no better than any of them! I know this because they're telling me. Each and every one. Expressing their true, unfiltered opinions of me and my pyramids, policies and skin tone.

I hear a *pop* from outside. Fireworks? It is a festive day or was going to be. Then I hear another *pop,* then an explosion.

Then more explosions and more *pops* and many, many more explosions.

"Ya really shagged the chook," President Kidman says telepathically. It's annoying having her in my head, but I can at least understand her now, even if she did just accuse me of fucking a chicken.

I open my mouth to speak, but nothing comes out except drool, which is something I would ordinarily not reveal, but now everyone knows because everyone knows everything.

"Check ya mobile, guv," President Kidman says, as it were, in a sing-songy voice.

I fart loudly as my body relaxes, and everyone knows because everyone knows everything.

"Stop stalling! Check it!"

I do. "What am I looking for?"

"Ya got Boomy?"

"The nuclear warhead tracking app? Why would I..."

Then it hits me. I don't need to check Boomy. I already know the world's full nuclear arsenal has been launched. Every bioweapon unleashed. Every killer robot turned on. As every human being, living or dead, goes bat-shit insane, in one way or another, at once, high up in the electromagnetic field.

I rip off the helmet and quite a lot of hair and toss it violently against an orb which shatters, but it's just a storage orb. The damage has been done. We are all inexorably connected, and it did not go as I planned. I truly believed merging all minds would foster global unity through empathy, but I was a fool. There are limits to connection's utility. Perhaps conjoined twins face long odds for a reason. Perhaps regular twins become creepy upon reaching adulthood for a reason. All I know is, we're not long for this world, the physical one, and that which awaits us is going to suck.

Then a tiny voice cries out amidst the din, and though it is quiet and meek, I hear everything now. It's Ronald. Poor little guy. And though I can't tell if he's living or dead, it's a trivial distinction at this point, he seems to be the only one not, as it were, shouting. His voice is calm. Soothing. He's not afraid. He's not angry. There is nary a molecule of judgment in him, even though he feels and sees what I feel and see, if not at my level. He whispers something, as it were, articulating a thought that, were I standing, would bring me to my knees like a cane to the hamstrings.

The meaning of life.

A secret as old as time that, once revealed, seems obvious. Like the name of that actor you were trying to remember, then it comes to you days later in the shower. David Koechner! This knowledge (of the meaning of life) is an injection of pure tranquility. The moment-to-moment anxiety that keeps me on time? Gone! The mental reflection upon and projection of interactions that don't matter or won't happen? Gone! Wearing a false mask forged in the fires of constant expectation? Gone! And I sure as shit don't care where my cell phone is, even though I do know.

A shadow passes over me, and I'm fine with it because I'm fine with everything now. It's President Kidman, no surprise, but she looks different somehow. Then it hits me. "Are you wearing a raincoat?"

"Yes, I am, Docta."

"And, uh, is that a knife in your hand or...?"

"Yes, Docta. A Bowie knife. Named for John Borwing, bloody rippa' Aussie bush cobba' he was hahaha."

"So... what are you going to do with it?"

She doesn't answer. Just lunges, roaring, pointed teeth bared. I brace for impact, but it doesn't come because she is tackled. Hard. It's Ronald! Coming to my rescue, and she's sent sprawling. The knife flies from her hand, punctures a nearby orb – and it's a functional one. Sparks fly, blue like the lightning, and she stumbles back-peddling into it and is electrocuted, her remaining hair standing up comedically before falling to her shoulders as she does the floor.

"Ronald!" I cry.

"I'm right here, boss!" he says, dragging himself to the dentist's chair, which I am too overwhelmed to budge from.

Ding! It's a notification from Boomy.

"Come here, old friend," I say, extending my arms, and Ronald climbs onto my lap, soaking me and my dark blue Ralph Lauren Purple Label single-breasted two-button suit in blood in the process but I don't care. It's already stained the color my face should be. "Thank you for saving me, good friend."

"We still gotta get to Buffalo, right?"

"That's right, Ronald. We sure do."

He coughs, speckling my power tie with blood. "Is there gonna be milk and honey when we get there?"

"Yes, my friend. All you can drink."

He smiles, coughs again. "It's okay, sir. I know we're never gonna go."

"Don't say that! Please, don't."

"We had a good run, didn't we?

"We sure did, Ronald. We sure did."

"How long you think before the missiles get here?"

"I don't know, Ronald. Let me see."

I check Boomy and-

(*static*)

ABOUT THE AUTHOR

Dr. Adam Tomlinson earned his PhD in science from The University of Science, an institution as esteemed as it is secretive, with a sprawling, forested campus, several major particle accelerators and whose graduates dominate the reputable scientific scene today. Dr. Tomlinson is a highly prolific author and sportsman, best known for his books on dendrochronology and campaign to have jousting included in the summer Olympic Games. He is unmarried. His father is Paul, his mother, Barb. He has a sister, Becky, an estranged twin brother, also named Adam, and is probably responsible for the end of the world.

NOTES

Made in the USA
Las Vegas, NV
13 December 2021

37524799R00109